Traveling Circus
and the
Skeleton Key

Ingar Rudholm & Jean Davis

Copyright © 2021

All rights reserved.

ISBN: 9781944815776

Dedication

To all the readers out there, I wanted to say thank-you for enjoying the Traveling Circus Trilogy. I enjoy traveling all over Michigan meeting you at book events. It has been a blast

Acknowledgements

Edited by Kelsey Turek
& Joan Young

A special thanks to Donald Ingersoll
for your continued support.

1

Whitehall High School, Michigan

As if there were an invisible paintbrush, the drawing turned from charcoal to color. The stem and leaves filled with green, and the petals bloomed red. Flynn plucked the flower from the paper, smiled, and handed the rose to Rena. Her cheeks blushed the color of the petals.

"Do want to go out sometime?" Flynn asked.

"I'm only 15." Rena sniffed the rose and then sighed. "My parents won't let me go out until I'm a sophomore, when I turn 16."

"Oh, okay."

"But we can be friends," she replied.

"I would like that," Flynn said with a wide smile.

"I'll write down my number," Rena said and scribbled in her notebook.

She tore the sheet of paper out of the book and handed it to Flynn.

"Thanks," he said. He felt as if he were floating in the clouds.

"See you tomorrow," Rena said as she gathered her books and walked out of the classroom.

"See you later," Flynn said as he rolled up the poster he created for the circus and put it into his back pack. The poster would make a good addition to his art portfolio when he applied for college.

I can hang it over my bed, Flynn thought.

⁓

Without his bike, Flynn walked home from school. After Salvatore's arrest, Flynn forgot his bike with the police. With a spring in his step, Flynn felt good being far away from the ringmaster and the circus.

Maybe my life will go back to normal.

The straps on his backpack dug into his shoulders as though he carried the weight of the past.

Why does it feel so heavy? I don't have that much homework, he thought.

When he readjusted the weight, he heard rustling inside the bag. The fabric of the backpack expanded like a balloon and the seams began to pop. A sharp object poked into the center of his back.

He shrugged the backpack off his shoulders and heaved a sigh of relief when he dropped it to the ground. He tugged at the straining zipper. It, too, seemed to sigh as it gave way. Inside, the body of the rhinoceros squirmed on the poster and the horn pierced the fabric of his backpack. The image of the lioness, Salvatore, and the pocket watch rippled.

Oh no, the poster is turning into real life! What do I do now? STOP! DON'T BECOME REAL! Flynn's inner voice shouted.

His mind raced and his vision started to spin.

Destroy the poster! But how?

Normally, his drawing became real in less than a minute.

Why was it taking longer this time?

Flynn imagined the rhinoceros causing chaos in the neighborhood and he would be stuck paying to for it. He tried zipping the backpack closed, but the animal was growing large and the ripples covered the entire paper.

Clutching the backpack to his chest, he sprinted home. With narrowed eyes, he focused all his energy and imagination to suppress his powers, but nothing worked. The backpack grew heavier as he rounded the mailbox and raced up his driveway.

Flynn dropped the bag into the burn barrel, burst into the garage, and searched through his dad's tools. He found a can of gasoline next to the mower and some matches on the work bench. He ran back outside, doused the backpack with gas, and lit the match.

POOF!

Bright orange flames devoured his bag and the circus poster. Purple smoke billowed skyward and disappeared. Dumfounded, Flynn gazed at the smoldering ashes.

Why can't I control my powers? Flynn wondered.

Out of the corner his eye, Flynn noticed something jumping up and down along the edge of the driveway. The white fluffy animal sprinted into a nearby bush. Curious, Flynn went over to investigate. Shivering under the shade of the leaves, a tiny bunny sat on its hind legs.

Is that from my poster? I hope the other animals didn't escape my drawing!

He scooped the rabbit into his arms and carried it into the garage. He found a box, laid an old rag on the bottom, and set the rabbit inside.

I'll take care of it until the circus comes back, he thought.

∼

Flynn's mom, Georgia, entered his bedroom after a quick knock. Her brown hair was pulled back in a ponytail and she wore a dress with a floral pattern.

She held out a business card and said, "I was doing laundry and I found this in your pants pocket."

The bold print on the colorful card read, "John Copley, Professor, Grand River Art and Music College."

"Who's that?" Georgia asked.

"I met him a while back when I made posters for the circus. He liked my artwork and he wanted to see my portfolio."

Georgia smiled, her gaze darting over to the old drawings on Flynn's walls. "That's wonderful news. At least something good came out of the whole ordeal."

"Maybe not," Flynn groaned.

"What do you mean?" Georgia said.

"Remember at the police station I showed you and Dad that my drawings turn into real objects?" Flynn asked.

"Yes," Georgia said.

"I don't know how to control my power," he said with a crackle in his voice.

She rubbed her forehead and sat down on the edge of the bed.

"You're right," Georgia said. "You can't use your drawings for the competition if they'll become real."

"How can I control my powers?" Flynn asked.

She rocked back and forth, biting her thumbnail.

"We'll think of something," Georgia said, looking up at him and tilting her head sideways. "Call the professor and hear what he has to say."

Flynn nodded.

Before his adventure with the circus, his parents wouldn't have approved of an art college as a career path. And the thought of picking up the phone and talking to someone he barely knew would've filled Flynn with anxiety. But now, he wasn't afraid to talk to people. Emboldened by his new inner courage, Flynn sat down on the couch, picked up the phone, and dialed the number on the business card.

"Hello, could I talk to Professor Copley, please?"

A man on the other end of the line answered, "This is Copley. How can I help you?"

"My name is Flynn Parkes. We met when I was hanging up circus posters in Grand River."

"Ah, yes. I remember you. You're very talented."

"Thank you." Flynn smiled and straightened his shoulders.

"How can I help you?"

"I want to apply for the scholarship you mentioned," Flynn said.

"Great. We host a yearly talent competition for high school students from around the state of Michigan," Professor Copley said. "We accept paintings, sculpture, photography, and music."

"Music?" Flynn said, raising his eyebrows. "My friend Rena plays music."

Flynn's thoughts stuck on Rena. *Can she control her powers?* He'd have to ask her.

Sammy and Buster had never mentioned problems with the powers Salvatore had given them. But Cordelia didn't seem to have control over hers either. She turned into a mermaid every night at sunset whether she wanted to or not. And Marcel, he grew huge every time he worked out. Their powers had sidelined both of their plans for the Olympics. Flynn hoped his powers didn't end his dreams, too.

"Both of you can apply," the professor said. "What grade are you in?"

"I'm a freshman," Flynn said.

"The competition is only open for sophomores, juniors, and seniors. But I'll put you on my list and mail you the information so you'll be ready for next year."

"Thanks." Flynn relayed his address and said goodbye.

Letting out a sigh, he hung up the phone and pondered his next move.

He didn't want to tell anyone his secret, but he needed someone to talk to.

Rena will understand, he thought. *She knows about my powers.*

He dialed Rena's number.

"Hello." Flynn spoke into the receiver. "Is Rena there? Okay, thanks."

There was a silent pause and then he heard shuffling feet.

"Hello?" Rena asked.

"Hey, Rena. It's Flynn."

"Hi," Rena said with pep in her voice. "I was just thinking about you."

"Really?" A smile spread across Flynn's face.

"Yeah, I was just thinking about all the crazy things we saw at the circus. Giants, mermaids, lions."

"Yeah, tell me about it," Flynn said.

"What's up?" Rena asked.

"The reason I called was because I have some good news and bad news."

"Oh no, what now?"

"I just talked to a professor over at Grand River Art and Music College. The college has a scholarship competition open to sophomores. I'm going to apply next year."

"That's great news," she said.

"I figured you might want to apply for the music scholarship."

"Yeah! Good idea," Rena said. "Thanks for letting me know."

"No problem."

"What's the bad news?" Rena asked.

"I can't control my powers. I can't stop my drawings from becoming real."

"Oh no," Rena groaned. "How are going to draw stuff for art class?"

"I don't know. Have you tried using your powers yet?" Flynn asked.

"Not really," Rena said. "Just in band class…Oh no…Wait… A few people in class started dancing. So I stopped playing the drums."

Flynn heard Rena's phone drop onto the floor.

Concerned, Flynn asked, "Rena, are you okay?"

He heard a muffled sound and then heavy breathing.

"Yeah, I'm okay," Rena said after regaining her composure. "What if I can't control my powers, too?"

"I don't know…"

2

Siren Bay, Michigan

Cordelia chewed on her fingernails and her foot tapped on the floor. She sat in the living room in her grandpa's cabin and stared at the newspaper on the coffee table.

The headline read: *Circus Steals Money from Local Business Owners.*

Below the article, she noticed a familiar name in the obituary. She picked up the paper and read it.

Viktor Rusalka, age 90, died in Leviathan Prison in Siren Bay. Rusalka is survived by his wife Ursula and his daughter Shirley. Viktor also has two sons, Rio and Murphy, who are each serving an eight-year prison term for kidnapping.

Cordelia laid the newspaper on the table and stared into space.

Good! Viktor is gone! she shivered. *He won't be bothering us anymore.*

The front door creaked open. Albert wearily strolled in. His pants and shirt were wrinkled from the long hours at the police station. He sat down in the recliner across from her and let out a long sigh.

"How did it go?" Cordelia asked, not sure if she wanted to know the answer.

"Well..." Albert said in a solemn tone. "The district attorney has agreed to prosecute only Jack and your dad. No other charges were filed against us or the other circus performers."

I can't believe my dad is in jail, Cordelia thought. A mixture of sorrow and relief flooded her mind. *He was a good person before the pocket watch. I don't want to become a monster like him.*

After the watch was destroyed, she started remembering all the bad things that had happened. She felt betrayed by all her dad's lies and promises. Jack and her dad deserved to be in jail, but it wasn't the outcome she wanted. She missed her dad even though he had changed. She wanted her normal life back and cursed the Secret Talent Scroll for all her problems.

"Your dad wants to talk to me," Albert said. "But I didn't visit him. I'm too angry with him."

"Me too," Cordelia nodded. "When he first came back, he said he had a plan to bring Mom back and fix the mermaid curse."

"What? How?" Albert asked, raising his eyebrows. "Why didn't you tell me?"

"I'm sorry," Cordelia said. "He wanted me to keep it a secret because you would never go along with the plan."

"Of course not," Albert said. "Why did he steal the money?"

"I don't know," Cordelia said. "He never told me. He just kept saying, 'Trust me.'"

Albert wrung his hands and said, "Our reputation is ruined here, but we can still perform in the south. So, I decided to move the circus to Florida and work the circuit down there. We'll have a fresh start."

With teary eyes, Cordelia looked around the room. A photograph from her swim practice hung on the wall and her trophies sat on the bookshelf. All the memories of her home and dreams of becoming a world class swimmer flashed through her mind.

She fought a lump in her throat and asked, "What about the Olympics? The crystal ball said Flynn would save the circus and help me win a spot on the team. But I'm still a mermaid. I don't want to give up my dreams."

Albert rocked back and forth. "I'll find a coach in Florida who's willing to train you. We'll figure something out."

"What about Marcel?" Cordelia asked.

Marcel had Olympic dreams, too, but the scroll had messed up all their lives. Searching her heart, she decided to forgive Marcel for prom and all his past mistakes.

"He needs to pay restitution for the car he wrecked when he helped break you out of the police holding cell," Albert said.

"He can't afford that," she said.

"I'll help cover the costs since he helped save you and the circus. If he wants to stay with us, he can keep his job."

She stood up from the couch, walked over to her grandpa, and gave him a hug. "Thank you, Grandpa."

"You're welcome."

"Where's the scroll and skeleton key?" she asked.

"I put them in a safety deposit box at the Shelby State Bank. I put both our names on the forms. Before we head south, you'll need to sign the paperwork. That way if something happens to me, you can access the box."

"Okay," Cordelia replied.

~

As Cordelia finished packing her suitcase she heard a knock at the front door of the cabin. Curious, she walked downstairs and heard muted voices coming from the kitchen. Rounding the corner, she saw Marcel sitting at the table talking with Albert. Without saying a word, Cordelia leaned against the refrigerator and listened.

"We're moving the circus to Florida," Albert said. "We're leaving this week."

Marcel's face turned pale and he fidgeted in his seat.

"Since my son tarnished the reputation of my circus, I'm letting everyone decide whether or not they want to stay," Albert continued. "Paula, Rego, Sammy, and Buster decided to move to Florida with Cordelia and I. They've already packed and left."

Looking down at the floor, Marcel nodded.

"I know Salvatore forced special powers on everyone," Albert said. "And he made them steal from people."

Marcel pressed his hands together and raised his fingers to his lips. "I have to tell you something."

"What is it?" Albert asked.

"I punched Flynn in the stomach because Salvatore wanted me to keep Flynn in line."

Albert crossed his arms and said, "Thank you for your honesty."

"I thought if I did something bad, then the spell could be broken," Marcel said, his foot tapped the floor. "But now, I feel guilty."

"Do you think you can control your anger now that Salvatore isn't here?"

"Yes, sir," Marcel replied. "Before he took over, I really liked working for you."

"You're a hard worker and I would hate to lose you," Albert replied. "But if you want to stay in Michigan and go to college, I would understand."

Lose Marcel? Cordelia's heart sunk. *What's Grandpa talking about?*

If Marcel stayed, this might be the last time she'd see him. He'd been by her side through thick and thin. Before he'd followed her dad's orders, he was a nice guy. They'd been good friends, maybe even a little more. But her dad had twisted them all. Now that her dad was gone, she hoped she could still be friends with Marcel.

"I'd like to go with you, if that's okay," Marcel said.

Filled with relief, Cordelia ventured over to the table and stood beside Albert.

"How would your parents feel about you moving?" Albert asked.

"I don't know," Marcel mumbled as his knee bounced up and down.

"If you want go with us, you'll need to talk to them," Albert said.

Marcel let out a long sigh.

Cordelia spoke up, "I don't know if it would help, but I can go with you for moral support."

Looking up at Cordelia, Marcel smiled and straightened his shoulders. "That would be great."

"Well, it's now or never. Go ask your parents," Albert said, gently shooing the two of them to the door.

Will his parents let him move to Florida? Cordelia worried as she tied her shoes and zipped up her jacket.

3

On the ride to Marcel's house, Cordelia stared out the window and memorized the oak trees, evergreen bushes, and picket fences. Soon she would be in another city, gone from the place she called home. She would miss Lake Michigan the most. Ever since she turned into a mermaid, water had become the fabric of her being.

"Thanks for going with me," Marcel said.

Cordelia nodded. "I would miss you if you didn't come with us to Florida."

"Really?" Marcel asked with a wide grin.

"Yes, really," she said.

As Marcel pulled into the driveway and parked the car, Cordelia saw two young boys wrestling on the ground in the front yard.

"Arghh," Marcel grunted. "My brothers are at it again!"

Marcel jumped out the car and ran over to the two boys. Cordelia cautiously followed, giving enough space for Marcel to confront the situation.

"Jacques!" Marcel shouted. "Get off him."

Marcel grabbed the tall muscular boy by the waist and tossed him to the side.

Jacques tumbled into a bush. His shirt was ripped, his blonde hair was frazzled, and he had grass stains on his faded blue jeans.

"Henri started it!" Jacques yelled, pointing to his younger brother with short brown hair and a swollen eye.

Henri stood, waved his thin arms, and stammered, "Liar."

Marcel shook his head and said, "Enough! I don't care who started it. You need to talk it out instead of fighting."

Cordelia's mouth opened slightly and she was surprised by Marcel's response.

Wow! Marcel has changed, she thought.

She remembered when Marcel jumped into a fight with Kyle, his friend from high school. She recalled how he treated Flynn. In the past, Marcel had let his anger get the best of him.

"Who are you to talk?" Jacques said, sticking out his bottom lip.

"Yeah," Henri said with bulging green eyes. "You're always the one starting stuff."

Marcel placed his hands on hips, puffed out his chest, and said, "That's the old me."

Jacques and Henri laughed and shook their heads.

"Sure," Jacques snickered. "We'll see how long that lasts."

"Go find something else to do," Marcel said. "Or I'll get dad out here."

Jacques wandered over to the garage, picked up a wayward basketball, and began to shoot some hoops. Henri took off on his bike and rode down the sidewalk while there was still daylight.

Looking at Cordelia, Marcel said, "Little brothers."

She tilted her head to the side and shrugged one shoulder.

Marcel took a deep breath and said, "Guess this is now or never."

They climbed up the porch steps, Marcel opened the door, and they stepped into the foyer of the home. Marcel called out to his parents.

"We're in here," Marcel's dad shouted.

Cordelia and Marcel meandered down a long hall and turned right into the living room. His dad was sitting in a recliner reading a newspaper and his mom was watching TV.

"Mom, Dad," Marcel said. "This is Cordelia."

Cordelia gave them a small wave and said, "Hello."

Mr. Duchamp's smile slowly faded.

Mrs. Duchamp turned off the TV and said, "Yes, I remember. You brought this young lady to your prom?"

"Yes," Marcel said. "She's the granddaughter of Albert. Albert is the owner of the Traveling Circus."

"Nice to finally meet you," Mrs. Duchamp said with a nod.

Mrs. Duchamp brown hair was held back with a clip and her full lips glistened under the recessed lights on the ceiling.

"Nice to meet you, too," Cordelia said as she sat down on the couch with Marcel.

"Hm," Mr. Duchamp said with a stiff upper lip. He set the newspaper on his lap and crossed his arms.

"Jacques and Henri were fighting outside in the yard," Marcel said.

Mrs. Duchamp rolled her brown eyes and asked, "Again?"

"Boys will be boys," Mr. Duchamp gruffly said, running his hand through his peppered grey hair.

Marcel scrunched up his face and shook his head.

"What's this all about?" Mr. Duchamp gave Cordelia a weary glance and then scowled. The crease on his forehead turned red.

Oh no, Cordelia thought. *Coming here was a bad idea.*

Marcel cleared his throat. "I know I've been in trouble lately and I need to pay for the damages. Albert has offered to help with the restitution payments."

"That's a relief," Mr. Duchamp sighed.

"But I need a job and the circus pays well. They're moving the circus down to Florida and I would like to go with them."

"Florida?" Mrs. Duchamp asked, raising her thin eyebrows.

"What about college?" Mr. Duchamp asked, leaning forward in his chair. "We agreed to let you postpone it for now, but you promised you'd start the winter semester."

Marcel's shoulders slumped and he looked at Cordelia for support.

Putting on a winning smile, Cordelia ignored Mr. Duchamp's scowl that was aimed at her and said, "Florida has plenty of colleges. I plan on taking some classes."

"Marcel is in trouble because of your dad!" Mr. Duchamp growled.

Cordelia's smile vanished and her knees trembled.

14

Traveling Circus and the Skeleton Key

My dad caused so many problems, she thought. *Now, I have to move away and I might lose Marcel, too.*

Marcel gave her an apologetic look.

Summoning all her nerve, she fought for her honor. "Yes. My dad is the reason we're moving, so we can get a fresh start. My grandfather runs the circus now and he's nothing like my dad."

Marcel nodded. "It's true. He's a good person."

Mrs. Duchamp raised one eyebrow and looked to her husband. He nodded the slightest bit and his frown faded.

"My grandpa will take good care of us, I'm sure," Cordelia continued, sitting a little straighter.

Giving Marcel a stern look, Mr. Duchamp said, "Whatever you're taking for your muscles, you need to stop. Your actions cost you a spot at the Olympics."

"Yes, sir," Marcel said.

Marcel had never told his parents the true nature of his strength, and Cordelia felt bad for using the scroll on Marcel. It was all her fault.

Marcel's parents glanced at each other as though they were having a silent conversation punctuated by nods and shrugs. In that moment, Cordelia missed her own parents and the way her dad used to be. The life she was supposed to have. Her stomach turned hollow.

Looking down at the scars on her knees, she thought, *The car accident changed everything.*

Marcel's face took on a determined gleam. "Please, I'll work part-time and go to college. You won't have to worry about me anymore."

"We'll always worry about you. You're our son," Mrs. Duchamp smiled sadly.

"Could you give us a moment?" Mr. Duchamp said. "Your mom and I need to discuss this in private."

"Yes, Dad," Marcel said.

Cordelia followed him outside.

∼

Cordelia stood on the sidewalk as Marcel paced back and forth on the front porch. "I don't think I've helped much."

"Sorry about my dad," Marcel grumbled. "He's a bit over the top."

"No, it's okay," Cordelia said, giving him a weary smile.

"And thanks for being here," Marcel said. "It made it easier."

"You're welcome," Cordelia said. Her smile slowly faded. "This might be goodbye."

Marcel stopped pacing and looked into her eyes. He gave her a worried look that melted her heart and brought back a memory from high school. His stern stare and rugged chin reminded her of the day he was suspended from school for fighting with Kyle. Marcel had tried to say something, but she couldn't hear his words.

If she didn't ask now, she might never know. "Can I ask you something?"

"Sure."

"When Coach John broke up the fight between you and Kyle, what did you try telling me in the hallway?"

He dropped his gaze and blushed. Before Marcel could answer, the front door creaked open.

Marcel's father peered outside and said, "You can come back in."

Looking at Cordelia, Marcel said, "I promise, I'll tell you someday."

They stepped back into the house and sat down in the living room. Marcel wiped his damp palms on his pants. Cordelia tapped her fingers on the arms of her chair.

"You were planning on going away to college, so I suppose you'd be moving out either way," Mr. Duchamp said. "We think it would be okay for you to go, but you need to keep up on your classes and restitution payments."

Marcel grinned. "I will, I promise."

Letting out a sigh of relief, Cordelia rested her hand on Marcel's broad shoulder. A warm feeling washed over her.

4

October
Whitehall High School, Michigan

Mr. Anders tapped his conductor's baton on the podium. Flynn stopped tuning his baritone saxophone and snapped to attention.

"Today," Mr. Anders said holding a sheet of music. "We're going to work on a piece by John Williams called 'Summon the Heroes.'"

Flynn looked over his shoulder at Rena. She nervously clutched her drumsticks and her cheeks turned red.

Flynn flipped through his sheet music and waited for Mr. Anders' cue. The music teacher waved his baton in the air and the students began to play.

When Rena started playing her drums, the other students began tapping their toes. Sarah, a tall blonde girl who played the clarinet, stood up in a trance and swayed to the music. A few other students stopped playing and started dancing, too.

Oh no! Flynn thought. *Rena can't control her powers. They can't stop dancing to her music!*

Rena abruptly stopped playing. Snapping out their trance, the befuddled students sat down in their chairs and murmured amongst themselves.

Scratching his head, Mr. Anders asked, "What is this all about? Some kind of prank?"

Traveling Circus and the Skeleton Key

"No," Sarah stammered. "I don't know what came over me."

"Excuse me," Rena said. "I need to use the bathroom."

Rena ran out of the room and didn't return until after the bell rang.

∼

Flynn's gaze jumped from Mrs. Hopper, his art teacher, to the classroom floor and then to the clock above the whiteboard. Wishing time moved faster, Flynn nervously tapped his foot and pushed his thin fingers through his blonde hair. He let out a sigh of relief when the final bell rang. He grabbed his backpack and scurried toward the door.

"Flynn!" Mrs. Hopper called out. "Can I talk to you for a minute?"

His sneakers squeaked on the tile floor as he spun around. With slumped shoulders, he dawdled over to Mrs. Hopper, who sat behind her desk.

Rena gave Flynn a worried look as she left the room with her friends.

"Why haven't you turned in your assignments?" Mrs. Hopper asked, tapping her fingers on her desk. "You're a great artist, but you're not applying yourself."

Flynn looked at the floor, unsure what to say.

Breathing in a big gulp of air, he thought *I need an excuse!*

"I thought you'd gotten over your shyness?" Mrs. Hopper asked.

Flynn avoided eye contact. "I'm sorry I haven't been doing my homework."

"I know you're not lazy, but if you don't put in the work, I'll have to give you a failing grade."

"No, no," Flynn pleaded. "Don't do that."

"What other choice do I have?"

With a knot forming in his stomach, Flynn asked, "Can you keep a secret?"

Sitting up straight, Mrs. Hopper asked, "What is it?"

He ripped a sheet of paper from his drawing pad, picked up a pencil sitting on her desk, and started a sketch.

"What are you doing?" she asked, raising her eyebrows.

"Just wait."

He set the drawing on her desk and the image slowly turned to color. A purple butterfly with black edges and white spots on the wings protruded from the paper. The insect flapped its wings and fluttered out an open window.

"What is going on?" Mrs. Hopper asked with wide eyes. She leaned back in her seat and rubbed her forehead. "That's impossible. Is this some kind of magic trick?"

"It's not a trick," Flynn responded. "Everything I draw becomes real."

His powers were out of his control and it was happening faster each time.

Mrs. Hopper stared out the window.

Flynn regretted revealing his power.

What if she tells everyone or kicks me out of class? he worried.

He leaned forward and asked, "Are you okay?"

"How did you do that?" she stammered.

"It's a long story, but it happened during my time with the circus."

There was a long awkward pause before Mrs. Hopper finally spoke. "Does anyone else know about this?"

"Just Rena and my parents. I thought it was neat at first, but now I can't control it."

"That is a problem," Mrs. Hopper said. "Be careful of what you draw until you figure this out."

Flynn nodded.

"You can turn in your assignments privately, that way you can keep up on your homework. Does that sound okay?"

"Yes, thanks," Flynn said. "But there's more."

"More?" Mrs. Hopper said, bracing herself for another surprise.

"I want to apply for a scholarship to Grand River Art and Music College. There's an art competition next year, but I don't know how I'm going to compete."

"Hmmm," Mrs. Hopper said. "Have you tried using a different

media instead of a regular pencil?"

"I'll try anything," Flynn said.

Feeling relieved by her willingness to help, his throat tightened and his eyes started to tear up.

Mrs. Hopper went over to the art supply closet, opened the door, and rummaged through a stack of paint tubes, colored pencils, and brushes.

She handed Flynn a box of markers. "Our next assignment is to draw a still life. Try these."

"Okay," he said as he walked out of the art room.

Carrying a little hope, Flynn shuffled down the empty hall. He heard someone calling his name. He spun around to see Rena running toward him.

"I was waiting for you," she said. "I need to talk to you."

"Sorry," Flynn said, staring at the floor. "I was talking to Mrs. Hopper."

"What did she say?" Rena asked.

"I told her about my powers."

Rena placed her hand on her forehead and groaned.

"It's okay," Flynn said. "She took it pretty good. She's letting me turn in my assignments in private."

"Lucky," Rena said. "I'm not telling anyone my secret. You saw what happened in band class. I've even tried using different drumsticks."

"What about a different instrument?" Flynn asked.

"Maybe that'll work," Rena said with a furrowed brow.

∼

Walking up the driveway, Flynn heard the sound of the circular saw. As he approached the open garage door, he noticed sawdust flying everywhere. His dad, Ray, was building a small rabbit cage out of chicken wire and two-by-fours.

Ray set his hammer on the work bench and smiled.

"What do you think?" Ray asked.

"Looks great," Flynn said and admired the cage.

"Having a pet is your responsibility," Ray said. "You gotta clean the cage and feed your rabbit."

"I will. Do you need a hand?"

"No, I'm almost done."

"Okay," Flynn said.

Flynn gathered some flowers from his mother's garden and carried them into the house. The flowers were brown and faded from the cold fall weather. He grabbed a bowl of blueberries from the kitchen, a vase for the flowers, and headed upstairs to his bedroom.

His old drawings of comic book heroes and images from his imagination hung on his bedroom walls. Before meeting Albert, he had created a fantasy world. Now, his dreams collided with reality and he had to sort the two out.

I wish I could draw a world where I could just disappear, he thought.

Setting the bowl of fruit and vase on the corner of his desk, he sat down, pulled a few markers from the box, and began drawing the still life.

When he finished, he squeezed his eyes shut and focused all his energy on suppressing his powers. A bead of sweat formed on his brow. When opened his eyes, his heart sank into his stomach. The vase and fruit bowl had pushed through the paper.

"Darn it!"

He gripped the marker, slammed his fists on the desk, and gritted his teeth.

SNAP! The marker broke in two pieces.

5

December
Whitehall High School

Mrs. Hopper kept close tabs on Flynn. Every week, after everyone left school, Flynn would drop off his homework so she could grade his art in private. She guarded his secret and never asked him to draw anything during class.

He placed the drawing of the fruit bowl and vase onto her desk. The image stuck out from the paper like speed bumps.

"You have a keen sense of detail and precision in your work," she said with admiration as she plucked a few blueberries from the bowl and ate them. "Yum."

Flynn sighed with a heavy heart. "What happens in college? I can't tell every professor my secret."

"You're right," she said, rubbing her forehead. "Let's try something else. Come with me."

He followed her to the art supply closet. She pawed through different items and then settled on some brushes and watercolors.

Handing him the box, she said, "Try these over Christmas break."

"Okay," Flynn said, shrugging his shoulders. "I'll try."

Discouragement hung over his head like a storm cloud. As Flynn shuffled toward the door, Mrs. Hopper wished him a Merry Christmas.

He mustered a cheerful, "You, too."

Walking into the hall he saw Rena leaning against the lockers with her head hanging low and her eyes were red.

Flynn cautiously approached her and asked, "Are you okay?"

Wiping away a tear, she said, "I tried playing a guitar, a clarinet, and a keyboard at home. But my parents started to dance as though they were in a trance. What am I going to do now?"

Resting his hand on her shoulder, he said, "We'll figure something out."

"Next semester, I'm taking a break from band," Rena said. "Mr. Anders is letting me do an independent study to work on the music competition."

"I'll miss hearing you play," Flynn said.

"We still can hang out in art class."

Flynn nodded as they walked down the hall together.

～

The wrapping paper was thrown away and the Christmas lights were turned off. Flynn filled a jar with water, went upstairs, and sat down at his desk. Staring at the color palette, images of Lake Michigan popped into his imagination.

Time seemed to stand still as he worked on his drawing. Taking a break, he leaned back and looked at his creation. The rolling waves in his painting slowly turned to a giant puddle and dripped onto the floor. He crinkled the soggy paper into a ball and threw it into the trash can. He grabbed a towel from the bathroom and cleaned up the water. Frustrated, he crawled into bed, turned off the light on the nightstand, and stared into the darkness.

Should I give up?

Feeling determined, he vowed to try something else. He wasn't ready to quit.

～

May
Holland, Michigan

As the school bus careened around the corner, Rena accidentally bumped into Flynn's shoulder. A warm feeling ran up his arm and into his heart. She gave him a smile.

Mrs. Hopper took all the art students on a school field trip to Holland to visit a local museum. Flynn and Rena had spent the whole day together laughing and talking.

Mrs. Hopper turned around in her seat and announced, "Before heading home, we're stopping by the Tulip Time Festival."

Rena looked at Flynn and said, "Cool, this should be fun."

"Your art assignment for today is to draw something in your sketchpad," Mrs. Hopper said as the bus pulled into the public parking lot. "You'll have one hour to complete your project. Then we'll pack up and head back to school for the day."

The bus creaked and groaned as it parked in a long space near the gardens. Gathering their supplies, the students chattered and exited the bus.

Mrs. Hopper pulled Flynn aside, handed him a box of pastel chalk, and said, "Maybe these will work."

With a weary nod, Flynn took the box.

The art students followed Mrs. Hopper along the sidewalk toward Windmill Island. They crossed over a pedestrian bridge and entered the 36-acre garden. The tulips were in full bloom and an apple-like smell filled the air.

Rena sat cross-legged in the grass in front of a long row of flowers. Noticing a butterfly land on a purple tulip, she began her sketch. A few feet away, Flynn found a wrought iron park bench next to a gazebo. He took a seat by himself and placed the sketchpad on his knees. In the sea of purple flowers, a white tulip stood out near Rena's feet.

"Can I draw the flower next to you?" Flynn asked.

Glancing over shoulder, Rena smiled and said, "Sure."

Tilting her head back, she breathed in the spring air and let the sun warm her cheek. The blades of the DeZwaan windmill turned in the breeze behind her.

Inspired by the moment, Flynn sketched the single white tulip.

Mrs. Hopper walked around the garden with a camera, taking pictures of the flowers and admiring all the students' drawings. She stopped when she reached Flynn.

"Rena," Mrs. Hopper said, while aiming the camera in her direction. "Smile."

Rena looked up with a grin. The camera clicked and snapped a picture.

Distracted, Flynn felt his sketchpad vibrate. Looking down, he saw the white tulip and stem protrude from the paper. He slammed the drawing pad closed and looked around.

Oh no! Did anyone see it? Flynn wondered.

With brooding eyes and slumped shoulders, Mrs. Hopper rested her hand on his shoulder.

"You tried," she whispered.

"What's the point of having powers if I have to hide it?" Flynn mumbled.

6

June
Whitehall High School

Flynn remained in his seat as the final bell rang. The other students dashed out of the art room laughing and cheering because it was the last day before summer break.

Vinnie, the quarterback for the football team, looked over his shoulder and sneered. "Flynn, are you staying for summer school?"

Vinnie's friends chuckled and high-fived each other.

Flynn shook his head and rolled his eyes. "I need to talk to Mrs. Hopper."

"Whatever," Vinnie snickered as he darted out of the classroom with his friends.

The room fell eerily quiet. Mrs. Hopper walked over to the door and peeked into the hallway.

"The coast is clear," she said.

She closed and locked the door for privacy.

Flynn reached into his backpack, pulled out his assignment, and set it on the table in front of him.

"Here's my project."

The last assignment for the year was to draw a large cityscape using linear perspective. His drawing turned into an architecture model of New York City, complete with skyscrapers and the statue of liberty. Flynn used an 8"x11" sheet of paper and the final model weighed several pounds. Luckily, no one questioned his bulging

Traveling Circus and the Skeleton Key

backpack. Using both hands, Flynn set the tiny city on the table and it landed with a thud.

Mrs. Hopper gasped. Her eyes widened as she examined the miniature city.

"Looks great!"

"Thanks," Flynn mumbled.

Placing his elbows on the tabletop, he rubbed both his hands on his face and groaned.

"What's wrong?" Mrs. Hopper asked.

"What about the art competition next year?" he whimpered through his fingers.

"I'm running out of ideas," Mrs. Hopper replied, wringing her hands. "Maybe you could try oil painting?"

Flynn gritted his teeth. "What if it doesn't work?"

"Keep trying," Mrs. Hopper said earnestly.

She went to the supply closet and grabbed a set of oil paints, three brushes, and brush cleaner.

"Try these," she handing him the supplies.

"Okay."

"Make sure you prime the canvas, first," Mrs. Hopper said.

Flynn nodded.

"And then lightly sketch your design with a pencil," Mrs. Hopper said. "Start out with dark tones and then proceed to lighter colors. Don't forget to clean the brushes with a rag and solvent."

She patted him on shoulder and gave him a weary smile.

"Good luck and have a good summer," she said.

"You too."

As he walked toward the door, he stopped and glanced at the wall full of photos. There were pictures of all his classmates and art projects. A picture of Rena from the Tulip Time Festival stood out amongst the images.

Mrs. Hopper walked over to Flynn and asked, "What are you looking at?"

Flynn pointed at the picture of Rena.

"You like her," Mrs. Hopper said with a wide grin.

Flynn blushed and shrugged his shoulders.

Mrs. Hopper unpinned the photo from the wall and handed it to Flynn.

"You can have it," she said.

Tucking the photo in his shirt pocket, Flynn smiled. "Thanks."

Flynn waved goodbye and ducked out the classroom door. In the hall, two sophomore boys, Alden and Jaxon, approached Flynn. Alden's sandy windswept hair bounced with each step. Jaxon strode down the hall. He was tall with black spiked hair.

Alden straightened his broad shoulders and said, "Hi Flynn."

How did they know my name? Flynn thought. He recognized the boys from pep rallies, but he'd never spoken to them before.

"Hi guys," Flynn acknowledged them with a nod. "What's up?"

Jaxon reached into his black trench coat pocket and held up a newspaper with the front-page headline that read, "Circus Steals Money from Local Business Owners."

"Were you kidnapped by this circus?" Alden asked.

Flynn felt lightheaded, unsure how to respond.

"We're not making fun of you," Alden said in a reassuring voice. "We're just curious."

"Why?" Flynn asked.

Flynn was skeptical about their intentions, but he would rather stickup for himself than slink away from any confrontation.

"My parents own an antique and repair shop on Colby Street," Alden said.

"Yeah," Flynn said. "I've seen it before."

"My dad bought some old circus equipment from a police auction," Alden said. "I think we found some stuff that belonged to the ringmaster."

Flynn's eyes widened and his forehead began to perspire.

"Maybe you can help us figure out what it all means?" Jaxon asked.

"Yeah," Alden said. "Can you give us the backstory on some of the stuff?"

"I don't know," Flynn said. "I'm trying to put that behind me."

"We can make it worth your while," Alden bargained. "We could trade something from the shop for any information you can give us. What do you need?"

Flynn rubbed his forehead and pondered the offer.

"Well, I need a bike. I never got mine back from the circus."

"Small red bike with a bent handle?" Jaxon asked.

"Yeah," Flynn's eyes lit up.

"I've seen it at the shop," Jaxon said.

"Come on. Tell us your story and we'll get your bike back. Deal?" Alden held out his hand.

After a brief pause, Flynn shook Alden's hand and said, "Okay."

What did Salvatore leave behind? Flynn wondered.

7

Nash's Antique and Repair Shop sign hung over the front door of the brick building with glass storefront windows. Jaxon drove his rusty old car around to the backside of the building and parked in front of the garage.

Alden unfastened the padlock, opened the garage door, and flipped on the light. The fluorescent bulbs flickered to life. Flynn saw his red bike leaning on the back wall of the garage.

"There you go," Alden said.

"Thanks!" Flynn said.

"No problem," Alden said.

A food cart broken into several pieces sat in the corner of the garage. The edges were charred and the wheels were bent. Flynn recognized it from the circus. He remembered Marcel tipping it over and lightning striking the side when the police arrived to set him free.

Flynn followed Alden and Jaxon over to the pile of broken parts.

"My dad found this at the police auction," Alden said. He opened one of the storage compartments and reached inside.

Flynn's jaw dropped when Alden held up the melted pocket watch. The glass face was broken and the metal edges were bent out of shape.

"What happened to this?" Alden asked.

Flynn's shoulders quivered and his eyes widened.

Does it still control time? Flynn thought.

"I think I can fix it," Jaxon said.

"Jaxon works here at the repair shop fixing old stuff," Alden said.

"No, no, no!" Flynn stammered. "That's a bad idea!"

"Why?" Alden asked.

Flynn wrung his hands and paced back and forth.

I gotta stop these guys from fixing the watch? Flynn thought. *What if Salvatore finds it?*

"You need to throw it away," Flynn said, pointing to the watch.

"Why should we throw it away?" Jaxon said. "I can fix it."

"Yeah," Alden said. "What are you not telling us?"

Flynn didn't know these guys and he wasn't sure if he should trust them.

Maybe, I can save some money and buy it? Flynn thought. *Then I'll get rid of it for good.*

"We held up our end of the bargain," Jaxon said. "We gave you your bike back."

"All we ask is the story behind the watch," Alden said. "Please?"

"You'd never believe me," Flynn said.

"Try us."

"Well," Flynn began his story, leaving out a few minor details like having the ability turn drawings into real objects. He told them about how Salvatore controlled time with the watch and how it was destroyed by a lightning bolt.

Alden and Jaxon stood with stunned looks on their faces, making skeptical glances at each other.

"And that's what happened when I was taken by the circus," Flynn concluded.

Alden took a deep breath, shook his head, and said, "That's a crazy story."

"Yeah, I know. Can I buy the watch from you?" Flynn asked.

"I'll ask my dad how much he wants for it," Alden said.

"I don't have any money right now," Flynn said. "But I'm looking for a summer job. I'll save up some money or maybe my parents will buy it for me."

"Okay," Alden said. "I'll let my dad know. How can I get a hold of you?"

"I'll give you my number," Flynn said. "Do you have something to write on?"

Jaxon grabbed a pencil and notepad from the work bench. Flynn wrote down his home phone and gave it Alden.

"Here's my number, too," Alden said, handing Flynn a business card with the antique store's phone number on it. "If you don't hear from me, give me a call."

"Okay," Flynn said. "I will."

"Do you need a ride?" Alden asked. "Jaxon and I can take you home."

"No," Flynn said with smile. "I'll ride my bike."

"All right," Alden said. "We'll be in touch."

Alden grabbed an air pump from the work bench and pumped up the flat tires.

"Thanks!" Flynn nodded.

Flynn hopped onto his bike and peddled home.

I know! Flynn thought. *I'll draw the money when I get home. And then I can buy the watch.*

～

Flynn ran upstairs to his bedroom, grabbed his money jar on the bookshelf, and sat down at his desk with his sketch pad. He sifted through the change and found a five dollar bill. He picked up his pencil and began drawing the money.

He nearly jumped out of his skin when he heard a rapid knock on the bedroom door. He scrambled to hide his drawings. All his papers slipped out of his hands and fell onto the floor.

His mom called out, "Flynn, I'm home!"

He quickly kneeled down and gathered up the sketches.

Georgia popped her head into his room and asked, "What's going on? Didn't you hear me call you?"

"Sorry," Flynn shook his head and his face turned red. "You're home early."

"Yeah, work was slow, so my boss let me leave."

She looked down at the sketch pad. Her eyes widened when the five dollar bill pushed through the surface of the paper and became real.

"What's going on?" Georgia asked.

She bent over, picked up the five dollar bill, and held it up to the light.

"It's fake," she said. "It's missing three vertical five's to the left of Lincoln's portrait. Did you make this?"

Flynn held up his hands and said, "I'm sorry."

"Flynn," Georgia sighed and placed her hand on her hips. "You can't make counterfeit money. You'll get in trouble with the police."

Flynn gulped really hard and worried about being arrested.

Georgia ripped up the fake money and threw it into the trash can.

She wagged her finger in the air and said, "Don't make any more."

"Yes, Mom." Flynn looked down at the floor and hung his head low.

Georgia patted his back and said, "It's illegal."

Flynn nodded. He felt guilty for doing something wrong.

∼

End of August
Whitehall, Michigan

The paint brushes and cleaner sat, unused, on Flynn's desk all summer. A stack of blank canvases leaned against the bedroom wall. Several weeks of driver's training and a summer job cutting grass in his neighborhood occupied most of his time and energy.

I'm never going to win the scholarship. He thought as he lay in his bed staring at the ceiling fan. *Should I even go to college? What could I do besides art?*

Traveling Circus and the Skeleton Key

The world held so many possibilities, but he couldn't decide which path to follow. He heard the phone ring, footsteps on the stairs, and then a knock on the door,

His mom peeked inside his room and said, "Flynn, it's for you."

Flynn walked to the door and his mom handed him the cordless phone.

"Hello?"

"Hey, Flynn! It's Rena."

A smile spread across his face and his heart beat a little faster.

"Hi Rena! How's it going?"

"Great! I've been working on my song for the competition by myself. How about you?"

His mood soured again at the lack of progress. He couldn't find the desire or the inspiration to create a painting.

"Not good," Flynn groaned. "Everything I've tried to draw comes alive. And I don't think the oil paints will work."

"That's a bummer," Rena said in soothing tone. "I called because I wanted to play you my song, but it sounds like this is a bad time."

"No, not at all," Flynn pleaded. He was ecstatic she had called and he didn't want to let her go so soon. "I want to hear it."

"Okay," Rena said. "Hold on, I'll set the phone down on the counter so you can listen."

Flynn heard feet shuffling and the clicking sound of Rena picking up her drumsticks. She started with a soft one tom-tom drum beat and then the music filled out with a bass drum and other tones. He imagined her drumsticks traveling all over her drum kit in an orchestrated pattern.

Kind of like painting, but with sound, he thought.

He tapped his foot to the beat and tried resisting the urge to dance. Her melody was catchy and upbeat.

Rena stopped playing, shuffled to the phone, and asked, "What do you think?"

"It sounded great!" Flynn was impressed.

"Were you dancing?" she asked.

"I started too. It was hard to resist."

"Arrrgh," Rena grunted. "I wish I could control my powers."

"You're going to create quite a stir at the competition, but I think you're ready."

"Almost. I need to practice with my bandmates and then we can record it. We'll be done soon."

Flynn sighed. "You're way ahead of me."

"I know you'll get there," Rena said. "Well, I'll talk to you when we get back to school, okay?"

"Sounds good, bye," Flynn said.

With slumped shoulders, he hung up the phone and stared off into space.

What am I going to do now? Flynn thought.

RING!

Startled, he nearly dropped the phone.

Raising the handset to his ear, Flynn said, "Hello?"

"Hi, can I speak to Flynn?" A male's voice crackled over the line.

"This is Flynn."

"Hey! It's Alden Nash from school."

"How's it going?" Flynn asked.

"Great," Alden said. "Jaxon and I fixed the pocket watch. It's good as new."

"I told you not to fix it," Flynn groaned.

"I can't sell a broken watch," Alden snapped back. "My parents want to sell it in their antique shop. But I figured I would give you first dibs."

Flynn rubbed his forehead and thought, *I need to destroy the watch.*

He looked across the room at the money jar sitting on his bookcase.

There goes my car fund money, Flynn thought.

"How much?" Flynn asked.

"A hundred dollars."

Letting out a long breath, Flynn said, "I'll take it."

"Great," Alden said. "We'll be back to school in a few days. I'll bring the watch and you can pay me then."

"Okay, thanks," Flynn said goodbye and hung up the phone.

Flynn went downstairs and handed the phone back to his mom.

"What's wrong, sweetie?" Georgia asked.

"I have a lot on my mind," Flynn said with sullen eyes.

"Are you worried about the art competition?"

"That and a few other things," Flynn sighed.

"Everything will work out okay," Georgia reassured him.

"I hope so," he said.

Georgia put her arms around her son and squeezed.

8

September
Naples, Florida

The sun sifted through the Venetian blinds, making the water in Cordelia's aquarium sparkle. She climbed out of her tank and prepared for the day.

A stack of unopened letters from her dad sat on her dresser. Salvatore had called a few times from prison, but Albert refused to accept the collect calls. After a quick breakfast, Cordelia stepped out of her motor home and inhaled the salty air.

She looked toward the small beach house Albert had bought after moving to Florida. The white trim and shutters stood out in the morning sun and the deep blue siding blended with the Gulf of Mexico in the background.

I miss our cabin in Siren Bay, Cordelia thought. *At least winter is warmer here.*

She felt like a real adult even though her grandpa lived nearby. She didn't mind having him check in on her every so often. She still had a family member that cared about her.

Marcel emerged from the beach house where he rented the quest bedroom from her grandpa. Marcel waved to her and they met each other at his car in the driveway.

"Sleep well?" he asked as they got in and buckled their seatbelts.

Cordelia shrugged. "The usual. You?"

"Up late studying." He backed out of the driveway and they

began the long drive to the community college campus.

"Lucky you. I have to study before sunset. Books and water don't mix. At least you don't have to deal with a mermaid tail! Not even the swimsuit can hide that."

Marcel nodded.

"We never seem to catch up," she mumbled.

Her grandfather packed in a ton of circus performances during spring and holiday breaks, leaving Cordelia and Marcel no time for a social life.

"Do you have practice today?" Marcel asked.

"Yes," Cordelia said. "After class."

"Okay, I'll wait for you," Marcel said, rubbing his forehead and staring down the road.

"Is something wrong?" Cordelia asked.

"It's just," Marcel's voice trailed off. "I wish I could train for the Olympics, too."

"Maybe you can try out again?"

Marcel sighed. "How can I pass the performance test? How can I work out without my muscles getting so big?"

"I don't know," she said.

"I wish there was some way to control the power running through my veins," he grunted.

"Yeah, me too."

"How come we can't control it?" he asked.

"I don't know how it works," Cordelia said. "It's like the energy can't be created or destroyed. It flows from one form to another."

⁓

Gulf Coast University

Cordelia shot quick glances at Marcel as they walked up the sidewalk to the front doors of the college.

Marcel opened the door for her and they walked inside the campus building.

"Well, I'll see you after your practice," Marcel said.

He turned and walked down the hall.

Cordelia wanted him to ask her out again, or at least show some interest. She would flirt with him or throw out hints, but he seemed content to just be friends.

After getting up early, swim training, and mending costumes for the circus performers, she was exhausted. All her energy had been tied up with her goals. She wished she had more time for dating. The only time she talked to Marcel was during the drive back and forth to college.

"Marcel," Cordelia called out.

He stopped in his tracks, turned around, and said, "Yes?"

"You have a good heart," she blurted out the first thing that came to her mind.

"Thanks," he said, holding his hand to his heart. "You too."

Marcel waved goodbye and then turned the corner of the hallway.

Disappointed, Cordelia headed to her class.

A few seconds later, Marcel reappeared.

He approached her, cleared his throat, and said, "I know this is a bad time, but maybe tomorrow, before sunset, can we go out on a date…or something?"

Her heart fluttered as she grinned. "Yeah, I'd like that."

∽

The sound of a whistle echoed through the auditorium. Dressed in a white t-shirt and gym shorts, Coach Neiman stood at the edge of the pool and held up his stopwatch.

"Way to hustle," Coach Neiman shouted, tapping his finger on the watch. His bushy black mustache flapped when he spoke. "Wrap it up for the day and I'll see you tomorrow."

With water dripping off her swim cap, Cordelia climbed out of the pool and looked down at her own waterproof watch. Her swim time was 54 seconds.

Still not good enough! Cordelia worried.

Every afternoon, she would meet with a trainer at the campus pool. She was part of a six-woman swim team at Gulf Coast University. Her time was getting better, almost up to Olympic-quality.

After practice, Coach Neiman's large hands gently pulled Cordelia aside. "The Olympic qualifiers are next month."

Cordelia's shoulders slumped.

One month? Already? How can that be?

"When?"

Coach Neiman raised his thick eyebrows, looked at his clipboard, and said, "According to my notes, they are at 8 pm on October 12. If you don't go, you'll miss your chance."

Cordelia had to figure something out soon. So far, she used her homework and performing in the circus as an excuse to leave early or miss training at night.

"You're an awesome swimmer," Coach Neiman continued. "But I can't arrange the training around your schedule. I'm not going to invest my time in someone who isn't fully committed."

Cordelia didn't argue with his point. "Yeah, I know."

With slumped shoulders, Cordelia trudged into the locker room and changed into her clothes. Walking into the lobby of the gym, she saw Marcel already waiting for her.

"Been here long?" she asked.

He shook his head. "How was your time today?"

"I'm doing better." She shifted her bag on her shoulder as they walked to the parking lot.

∼

During the whole ride home from practice, Coach Neiman's words echoed in Cordelia's mind.

How am I going to compete at night? she thought, staring out the car window.

"You've barely said anything since you got into the car," Marcel said, still keeping his attention on the road. "Are you okay?"

"I want to go home," she whispered to the window.

"We'll be back in Naples soon."

"That's not home."

"I know," he whispered. "You can talk to me, Cordelia. You know that, right?"

She nodded.

"Then what's wrong?"

Cordelia tore her gaze from the scenery to take in his worried glance.

"I found out the Olympic qualifiers are next month at night."

Marcel gripped the steering wheel, narrowed his eyes, and said, "What are we going to do now?"

"I need to break the mermaid spell. What if I do something bad so the spell can be broken?"

"No, you can't do that. Cordelia, you're not like your dad. I don't want you to change. You have a good heart."

If she wanted a chance to qualify for the Olympics, she was going to need more than a good heart. She needed a miracle.

"We'll think of something," Marcel said.

"I'll talk to my grandpa after dinner," Cordelia said. "Maybe he'll have an idea."

Marcel rubbed his forehead and sighed.

"I hope so," he replied, staring off into space. "We're running out of time."

9

Sitting alone in her motor home eating a turkey sandwich, Cordelia thought, *I wish my mom was here.*

Her mom had been gone so long that Cordelia was starting to forget what her mother looked like. She unlatched the chain from her neck, set the gold locket on the table, and opened it. The first picture showed Albert when he was much younger. His brown wavy hair made him look charismatic. The other picture showed her mom and dad holding Cordelia as a baby.

She missed having conversations with her mom about her training, school, anything really. She had two happy parents and dreams of becoming an Olympic swimmer. Now, her mom was gone and her dad was in jail. She felt as if she was chasing an impossible dream. She sighed heavily.

Who am I kidding? I'll never qualify for the Olympics. I should give up!

The thought of dropping out of training made her dinner roll around in her stomach. She imagined the looks of disappointment on everyone's faces if she gave up. Upset, she pushed the half-eaten sandwich away. She closed the locket and fastened it back around her neck.

No quitting! Cordelia shouted back at herself. *There has to be another way to fix things.*

Once again, an image of the second spell on the Secret Talent Scroll popped into Cordelia's memory.

If the person uses the power for evil, the spell can be broken.

The words echoed in her mind, twisting and turning.

Maybe I need to be "bad" so the spell can be broken, she thought.

Pushing away the negative ideas, Cordelia walked out the front door, down the steps to the beach, and leaned against a palm tree. A butterfly with purple wings landed on her shoulder.

Throughout the day, dark storm clouds had formed in the sky. Distant thunder rumbled and the palm trees swayed in the wind. Along the horizon, swirling clouds hovered over the Gulf.

Staring out over the ocean, she pondered the past. She blamed her dad and herself for all her problems. She reflected on all her decisions leading up to this moment. If she hadn't used the scroll, her life would be different.

Maybe my mom would still be alive? Cordelia thought.

A melancholy tune drifted through the air. Cordelia faintly remembered hearing the song as a child, but she didn't know the name.

Cordelia looked around in the direction of the music and saw her grandpa playing a harmonica while swinging in a hammock strung between two palm trees. When Albert noticed her presence, he abruptly stopped playing.

Looking away, he said, "I'm a little rusty."

"I miss hearing you play."

Albert tucked the harmonica into his shirt pocket and folded his arms. His eyes and nose were red.

"Is everything okay?" Cordelia asked.

"Today would've been my 50-year anniversary with Elsa," Albert said with a crackle in his voice. "I was playing our song."

"It's okay to play music again," Cordelia said, letting out a sigh.

With eyes filled with sorrow, Albert didn't respond. She knew he missed Grandma Elsa and the music they shared together was a painful reminder of their love.

Albert climbed out of the hammock, walked over to Cordelia, and put his hand on her shoulder.

"Someday, I'll play again," Albert said.

Pointing to the gloomy clouds, Cordelia said, "I hope it's not a hurricane."

"I've been keeping an eye on the news," Albert said. "According to the weatherman, the storm is supposed to pass by us."

"That's good," Cordelia said.

"How was your day?" Albert asked.

"My coach said that the qualifiers are next month and the competition is at night. How will I compete if I'm a mermaid?"

"Hmmm," Albert rubbed his chin. "I don't know. Let's see what the crystal ball has to say."

Cordelia shook her head. "It hasn't helped us so far."

"I used the crystal ball to find you when you were kidnapped," Albert reminded her. "And it showed us Flynn coming to save the circus."

"And look where that got it us."

"Come on," Albert pleaded. "Follow me."

Cordelia reluctantly followed him inside and sat down at the kitchen table.

"I'll be right back." Albert said, disappearing into his bedroom.

A few minutes later, he returned, sat in his chair, and placed the crystal ball on the table between them. Waving his hand clockwise over the crystal ball, they watched the purple smoke swirl inside the glass.

"What is in Cordelia's future?" Albert mumbled.

The smoke parted and a blurry image showed the two of them sitting at the kitchen table. Like a miniature movie screen, the image sped into the future, showing Cordelia winning a medal at the Olympics. Her dad and Albert were in the crowd.

The movie changed reels and flipped into an alternate future. The crystal ball showed a circus performance where Cordelia jumped off the high dive platform and splashed into a giant tank of water. As the crowd cheered, she ran to her camper and cried alone. The image faded and the smoke cleared.

Distraught, Cordelia stared at the empty crystal ball. "Why did it switch?"

"I don't know," Albert whispered. He waved his hand over the ball. "How can Cordelia achieve her Olympic dreams?"

Smoke swirled inside again, but instead of an image, a low voice came from the ball: "Cordelia needs to make peace with her father and the past before she can achieve her dreams."

"What is that supposed to mean?" Cordelia said, curling her lip.

"Maybe it means you have to reconcile with your dad," Albert said.

Leaning back in her seat, she pondered, *How can I forgive my dad when I'm still angry at him?*

"The crystal ball told us to use the scroll and I will swim again, but instead it turned me into a mermaid. Why should we trust it now?" Cordelia asked, slamming her fist on the table.

Albert remained silent.

"Nothing worked out like it was supposed to." She groaned. "Flynn was supposed to help me achieve my Olympic dreams. But he's back in Michigan, still in high school. He helped the circus, but he hasn't helped me. Maybe the stupid crystal ball got it all wrong."

"What other options do we have?" Albert pleaded.

Cordelia crossed her arms and said, "If I break Dad out of jail, I'll become a bad person. Then we can use the second spell to reverse the mermaid curse."

"No," Albert replied. "Bad idea. You'll ruin your chance at the Olympics if you're caught."

"My life is already ruined!" she raised her voice. Her face turned red and she clenched her fists. "I don't want to be stuck in the circus the rest of my life, like my dad."

Albert's face turned pale; she could tell she hurt his feelings.

"Your dad dropped out of college to make money to support his family," Albert whispered.

Cordelia's jaw dropped and her heart stopped.

"What are you saying?" she barely spoke the words. "It's my fault?"

"No, no, not at all," Albert begged her to understand. "I'm trying to say that your dad made the right decision and supported his family."

With tears in her eyes, she picked up the crystal ball and threw it to the ground. A bright flash and loud pop echoed through the house when it smashed into pieces. The walls shook and the windows rattled. Purple smoke escaped from the broken glass and swirled around the kitchen, and then it flowed into Albert's mouth.

Cordelia coughed as the purple smoke quickly crept into her nose and swirled around her neck. Her head felt fuzzy and the room began to spin. The locket around her neck felt warm and she watched the smoke wrap around Albert's wedding ring.

Fighting to catch her breath, she stormed out of Albert's house, marched into to her camper, and locked the door behind her.

Outside her window, the sun began to set behind the clouds. Coughing out the purple smoke, she changed into her swimsuit and slid into her aquarium as her legs fused together. Her fishtail churned the water and stirred the pebbles on the aquarium floor as she swam from one end of the tank to the other. Feeling trapped, she stopped swimming, crossed her arms, and floated to the bottom of the tank.

She heard a knock on the camper door and the faint sound of her grandfather calling her name. Ignoring him, she let anger stew until she fell asleep.

︵

A thunderous boom and a flash of light jolted Cordelia awake. Heavy winds rocked the camper back and forth, causing water to splash over the sides of the aquarium. Lightning flashed outside her window and the thundering booms made the walls and aquarium shake. Large raindrops pelted the roof.

BOOM! CRACK!

Suddenly, a tree crashed through the camper roof, ripped open a giant hole in the ceiling, and busted the aquarium wide open. The water gushed out, flooded onto the floor, and expelled Cordelia from the tank. She reached out for a steady object to grasp, but couldn't reach a solid object, instead she cut her hand on the broken glass of the aquarium. She bit her bottom lip and looked down at the gash in the palm of her hand. Blood streamed out of her wound and blended with the rain pouring through the collapsed roof.

"Help!" Cordelia gasped for air.

The camper door handle and the lock rattled.

THUD!

The door burst open after a heavy kick from Marcel's foot. Drenched in rain, Marcel stood nearly 12 feet tall as the hurricane winds tore at his clothes.

"Are you hurt?" he asked.

His muscles were huge from working out with his weights.

Clawing the floor, Cordelia crawled toward him as her tail dragged along the broken glass. Marcel reached his giant hand inside the camper, picked her up, and cradled her in his arms.

Looking over his shoulder, she watched the shutters and shingles snap off her grandpa's home. Branches and leaves sailed through the air and the storm pounded against the shore.

Fat raindrops plummeted from the sky and the swirling sand stung her eyes. Howling wind bent the palm trees like twigs and threatened to drive them both face first to the ground. Waves crashed on the beach, frothy and angry. A lightning bolt split a nearby tree in two pieces. Marcel ducked for cover as a branch landed with a thud next to his feet.

Holding Cordelia close to his chest, Marcel waded into the ocean. Waves pounded against their bodies. Fighting the current, Marcel walked out until he was waist-deep and then let her go.

"Save yourself!" Marcel pleaded.

"I don't want to leave you here to die," she said.

"Go!" Marcel shouted. "I'll find shelter."

He gently pushed her deeper into the water.

"Be safe!" Cordelia yelled. Her voice was barely audible over the howling wind.

Plowing through the tall waves, she swam out 200 feet and popped her head above the water. The salt water stung the open cut on her hand. She gritted her teeth. A stream of blood trickled behind her like a long string of red yarn.

"Watch out!" Marcel yelled.

Cordelia spun around. A sailboat with a broken mast and a bent rudder barreled straight for her. Without a captain, the steering wheel spun back and forth. The deck was missing a crew. With seconds to spare, Cordelia dove underwater. The hull of the ship skimmed over her head and smacked against her tail. Her fish scales stung from the impact.

10

Cordelia turned around and watched the dark shadow of the boat speed toward shore.

Oh no! she thought. *It's heading straight for Marcel!*

Thrashing her tail and arms, she propelled her body through the water faster than any of her swim competitions. She breached the crest of a wave and watched in horror as Marcel tried to swim out of the way. The sailboat smashed into his right arm, nearly knocking him unconscious. A giant wave crashed down upon his head. The sailboat kept moving forward and slammed into the beach. Water and sand shot into the air like a geyser. The fiberglass frame of the boat cracked and buckled.

She wiped her brow, dove underwater, and went to rescue Marcel. Sand and water churned in front of her face. With blurry eyes, she saw Marcel being tugged away by the riptide. She reached out to grab his arm, but her fingertips grazed his shoulder. He disappeared into the darkness.

Propelled by the current, Cordelia rocketed through the water. With speed and agility, she chased after him. After a few minutes, she finally caught up. Bubbles floated out of his nose and mouth. He gasped for help, but the sound was muffled by the water. His body and muscles shrank back to normal size as he sank. He'd been holding his breath for too long, even for his lungs. He was getting weaker by the second. Drowning, his eyes rolled back into his head and his body went limp.

She fought back her tears and summoned all her courage. Utilizing every muscle in her body, she scooped him up in her arms. She cocked her tail and swam upward. She tugged his body to the surface. The sky was dark, the wind was fierce, and she couldn't see the shore. The riptide had pulled them a long way from home.

Using her tail to keep them both afloat, she held Marcel's head above the surface. With one hand under his back, she tilted his head to one side, but he still wasn't breathing. She started mouth-to-mouth resuscitation.

Please breathe! she pleaded.

After a full minute, he sputtered, coughed, and worked the water out of his lungs. He slowly looked up at her with a tired smile.

"You need a doctor," Cordelia said.

Marcel looked down at his red and swollen arm and groaned, "I think it's broken."

They tossed and turned in the tall waves. Heavy winds and rain pelted Cordelia's face. If she were alone, she would've sought shelter at the bottom of the ocean.

"I'll take you home," Cordelia said with desperation her eyes.

He shook his head. "Don't worry about me. I'll slow you down. I'll swim home."

"I'm not leaving you alone."

Marcel was stranded, hurt, and far from home because of her.

I'm not like my dad, she thought. *I care about my friends and family.*

11

With the wind flipping through her long hair, Cordelia peered through the downpour and saw a small patch of blue sky moving west.

How could that be? she wondered, but then it dawned on her.

"Marcel, it's the eye of the storm!" Cordelia yelled, pointing to the sky.

"What should we do?" Marcel asked with fear in his eyes.

"We can ride out the storm in the eye"

"I can't swim that far," he groaned and rubbed his wounded arm. "Without my dumbbells, I can't pump up my muscles."

"Use your good arm to hold onto me. I'll swim for both of us."

Her shoulders tensed and tightened at the thought of carrying him so far. Mustering all her courage, she made a life-or-death decision. With the help of her tail, she would use her inner strength to travel the long distance.

Marcel looked up at the sky and back at Cordelia.

"The storm is heading north," Marcel replied. "If we head northwest, we might find the center."

Cordelia nodded. She wrapped one arm around his muscular chest and held onto him with a firm grip. Even though he had shrunk down to normal size, he still had big muscles.

Lying on his back, Marcel pushed through his pain and held his head above the water. Thrashing her tail, Cordelia propelled them through the water and struggled against the current. Swimming through the peaks and valleys of the waves made her stomach churn, and the salt water stung her eyes.

A wave crashed against Marcel's shoulders and he lost his grip. He tumbled backward into the waves. Cordelia made a sharp U-turn and went back for him. His arms flailed and his head bobbed up and down. Like a life preserver, she propped him up.

"Sorry," he said. "My hands slipped."

"I won't leave you behind," she reassured him. "Trying climbing onto my back."

He grabbed onto her shoulders and laid his chest against her back. She felt his body tremble and his muscles twitch. She pushed forward while he kicked his strong legs. Even with his help, her muscles were slowly wearing out. She had to get them to the eye of the storm before she lost her stamina.

Digging deep, she poured every ounce of energy into her tail, driving them through the giant waves. As time passed, she realized it wasn't enough. She slowed, turned her head, and yelled over the howling wind.

"I don't think I can make it."

With desperation in his eyes, he pleaded, "Leave me behind."

Her mind searched for answers to their problems as the waves tossed and turned their bodies. Gauging the speed of the clouds, she hoped they were near the center.

"I swim faster underwater," she replied. "I'll come up so you can catch your breath. Hold on, okay?"

He nodded and rested his forehead against her neck.

Cordelia dove underwater, bypassing the wind and the driving rain. She gained momentum and cut through the water like a shark, popping up every 30 seconds so Marcel could breathe. Even with the time to surface, traveling underwater was easier. She continued onward, pushing her aching muscles.

After plowing through several large waves, she entered into a pocket of eerie calm. The wind subsided and the waves were less choppy. Dark clouds swirled around them in a one-mile radius. Marcel shivered.

Cordelia relaxed her shoulders and let out a sigh of relief.

A jagged white piece of wood floated past them and then another. Cordelia flipped her tail, raised herself out of the water, and looked around.

"It's a sailboat," she said, pulling them both toward the wreckage.

"I wonder if anyone survived?" Marcel asked.

She turned her head and said, "I don't know."

Listening above and below the water, she didn't hear any cries for help. They didn't see anyone clinging to the floating debris.

"Did the waves carry them away?"

"Maybe," Marcel replied.

They searched for a life preserver or a lifeboat, but the ship was scattered into a million pieces. Marcel came across some rope and a large section of wood. Cordelia helped tie the rope around his chest and the chunk of wood so he wouldn't slip off. He gripped the makeshift raft and floated on the rolling waves.

"I'm tired. I need to rest," Cordelia said

She flipped on her back, looked up at the dark sky, and let her sore muscles rest.

"Why do we have such bad luck?" she asked.

Marcel shook his head. "I wish I knew."

"Me too."

Cordelia rested her chin on her arms.

"Will you be okay up here for a bit? I need to breathe underwater."

"Yes," Marcel said. "Thanks for getting us here."

"You're welcome. I'm sorry I've gotten you into this mess," she said before letting her body slip below the surface.

She made a mental note of the place where she'd left Marcel. Feeling distressed, Cordelia closed her eyes and sank downward.

Grandpa has to be worried sick by now, she thought. *I hope he found shelter. Marcel should be on land with the others, not stuck out here with me.*

As the water temperature dropped, she breathed in a rhythm, relaxed her body, and drifted with the flow of the current.

The locket around her neck turned warm, vibrated, and the cover unlatched. Her eyes popped open when something soft and warm grazed her arm. Several purple glowing orbs the size of quarters floated out of the locket, descended toward the ocean bottom like snowflakes, and disappeared into the darkness.

Am I seeing things? she wondered, rubbing her eyes. *Is that the smoke from the crystal ball?*

12

With the orbs leading the way, Cordelia swam into the depths of the ocean. The rocky bottom opened up to a deep canyon. Inching closer to the rim, she looked over the edge; the deep crevice appeared to stretch into infinity. Clicking with her tongue, she sent out sonar signals. Several seconds later the sound bounced back.

The current pushed her closer to the edge of the canyon. Frightened that she might fall into the abyss, she grabbed onto a rock formation. She peered into the darkness and the emptiness stared back at her. Frigid water sent chills down her spine. A sense of sadness and loneliness threatened to destroy her warm heart.

The current grew stronger and a giant shadow loomed above. She dug her fingernails into the rock and steadied her body. A whale skimmed overhead. Its massive tail swayed up and down. Clusters of white barnacles coated the rugged skin. A low click and whistle vibrated through the water as the whale glided through the water. Plankton schooled in its wake. Within seconds, the whale disappeared into the shadows.

The purple orbs spiraled over her head. Suddenly they collided into one another, creating a small explosion and a blinding flash of light. Cordelia covered her eyes until it faded into a dull glow. Curious, she lowered her hands.

A ghostly purple vision of her mother, Gala, floated before her.

Her mother's long hair danced with the current and a smile spread across her face. Cordelia reached out to touch her mom, but her hand pushed through the shadowy figure.

"I miss you," Cordelia whispered. Her tears blended with the salt water.

Gala whispered, "I miss you, too."

Cordelia's throat felt thick. "It's all my fault. If you hadn't taken me to swim practice, you wouldn't have died in the car crash and dad wouldn't be in prison."

"No, my darling," her mom said. "It's not your fault. Don't blame yourself."

Her mother's presence flowed around her in a loving hug. Cordelia missed her mother's touch, how she smelled, and the softness of her hair against Cordelia's cheek.

"I'm sorry, Mom."

"Don't be sorry. Death is a part of life. Even your dad, who had the power to control time, couldn't change the past. But you control your future with every decision you make," Gala said in a soft tone.

"But how?" Cordelia asked. "Every decision I've made has brought me bad luck. Using the scroll changed my life forever."

"Oh, my dear," her mother said. "You saw the scroll as a shortcut to achieving your dreams. Compete on your own merits rather than relying on the magic. Use your gifts to help others rather than helping yourself."

"Yes, I cheated, but I get mad when I don't get what I want. I let everyone down."

"You can't always control the outcome, but you can change how you feel about it. Learn to enjoy the journey," her mother replied. "Success will be much sweeter."

Cordelia bit her bottom lip. "How can I achieve my goals if I'm a mermaid?"

"Reconcile with your father and help him become a better person. You can save him."

"He betrayed me and hurt my feelings," Cordelia replied, feeling angry at the thought of her dad. "How can I forgive him after all he has put me through?"

"It's not going to be easy," her mother said. "He's willing to change. He's had time to think about his actions."

Cordelia let the words sink in, meditating on her mom's advice. She closed her eyes and breathed in and out. When she reopened her eyes, her mother's image began to fade.

"Don't go!" Cordelia begged.

"I'll always be with you," her mother said, holding her hand to her heart. "I love you."

And with her mother's last word, the image broke into several purple orbs and floated back inside Cordelia's locket. As the cover of the locket closed, she felt a warm sensation pulsate through her body. Even though her mother was gone, Cordelia felt her presence in her heart.

"Love you, too," Cordelia said. She knew her mom was listening... And always would be.

~

After a few hours, Cordelia popped her head above water and found the wind and storm clouds had subsided. She swam over to Marcel and gave him a weary smile.

"You saved me," he said. He held onto the wreckage and his body shivered.

She pushed his wet hair out of his face. "You saved me first."

"This isn't quite what I had planned for our first date."

Cordelia laughed. "I would hope not."

Whenever situations became stressful, they moved away from each other. It was time she got some answers.

"When you got into a fight with Kyle and you were suspended from school, what did you try to tell me in the hall?" Cordelia asked.

His bashful grin that made her insides go all mushy returned to his face. "I wanted to say that I love you."

As if a protective shield had been removed from her heart, she leaned in and kissed him.

It was the perfect end to a not-so-perfect date, she decided.

"I'm sorry you got hurt because of me," Cordelia whispered. "I let my anger get the best of me."

There, accepting responsibility isn't so hard, she thought. In fact, talking to him felt good.

Marcel had always been there for her. In the past, stressful situations had driven them apart, but they worked together this time. She took a deep breath and let it out slowly.

He tilted his head and said, "I'd like that." He squirmed around as if trying to find a comfortable position. "Everyone expects me to act tough and I'm not comfortable showing my feelings. I wanted to tell you a lot things, but I wasn't strong enough to say them."

"You can tell me anything," Cordelia said.

Marcel stared deep into her eyes, making her heart flutter and soften. She caught a glimpse of a warmer side to his hard exterior. She had to admit her muscles weren't the only things aching. Her heart and conscience were burning.

I hope grandpa will forgive me for smashing his crystal ball and running away, she thought.

"Do you have any energy left?" she asked, resting her head on his shoulder.

He nodded.

She swam to the edge of the abyss and survived without drowning. After finding some light in the darkness, she felt like she could handle anything. Tired and soaked, Cordelia helped Marcel swim home.

~

Naples, Florida

Cordelia and Marcel arrived before sunrise. Nearing the beach, the rolling waves were calm and the breeze was gentle. Trees had fallen down and broken branches littered the shore.

Cordelia let out a sigh of relief when she saw her grandpa's home still standing with minor damage, but their trailers were wrecked. Rego's camper sat upside down in the middle of the road. Her heart sank when she saw her trailer spattered with mud. A large tree stuck through it like nature had been playing a dart game. The place she called home was destroyed. There was no going back. Instead of relying on her dad or grandpa, she had to rely on her own determination.

I hope we can fix my aquarium.

Sammy and Buster cleaned up the fallen branches and stacked them next to the backyard fire pit. Paula and Rego were talking to a tow truck driver and a police officer about their damaged vehicle. Albert walked around Cordelia's motor home, rubbing his forehead and surveying the damage. He picked up a few broken shutters and carried them to his shed. When he remerged, he saw Cordelia and Marcel walking up the beach. His face turned pale as though he was looking at a ghost.

Albert ran to Cordelia and hugged her. "I thought I lost you."

"I'm sorry," Cordelia said, feeling guilty for their argument the night before.

With weary eyes and trembling hands, he let her go and stepped backward.

"Where have you been? I was worried sick. Paula and Rego flew up and down the beach looking for you."

"I'm sorry I broke the crystal ball and hurt your feelings." Cordelia gazed out at the shoreline. "After our argument, I needed to get away and clear my head. I was so upset."

"I know, sweetie. I'm sorry too," Albert said. "But you can't run off like that."

"I know, Grandpa," she sighed. She looked around, taking in all the damage. "I'm glad no one got hurt."

"It was terrible," Albert said. "We lost power and the wind destroyed most of the neighborhood."

"At least the hurricane didn't destroy your home," Cordelia said.

Looking at Marcel's arm, Albert said, "Let's go to the hospital and have a doctor look at your arm."

Cordelia nodded. "I'll go, too."

The emergency room bustled with nurses scurrying from one room to another. A doctor was in the examining booth bandaging Marcel's arm.

Biting her nails, Cordelia sat with Albert in the waiting room.

Albert leaned in close to Cordelia. "There's something I need to tell you."

Lowering her hands to her side, she asked, "What is it?"

"After you left, the smoke from the crystal ball gave me a vision of your Grandma Elsa."

"Really?" Cordelia gasped. "Mom visited me, too!"

Albert's eyes widened. He held up his left hand and showed her his wedding ring. The ring had a purple sheen that sparkled under the fluorescent lights.

"Wow," she whispered.

Pointing to her neck, Albert said, "Look at your locket."

Holding her breath, she unlatched the chain and held the locket in her hand. The gold color had changed to a light shade of purple.

"The power from the crystal ball must've fused with the metal," Cordelia whispered.

"Elsa said you need to visit your father," Albert said.

Cordelia's neck hairs stood on end. "My mom said the same thing."

"Last night before the power went out, I called your dad," Albert said, squeezing her shoulder. "He asked for you and he apologized for his actions. I know it's hard to forgive him, but he misses you. Despite being angry, he's still your father."

What am I going to say to him? she wondered.

Cordelia rubbed the locket with her thumbs. "Okay, but I don't want to go back to Michigan alone."

"I'll go with you," Albert said. "Paula and Rego can stay here and run the show while we're gone."

"What about Marcel? Can he go, too?" she asked, longing for moral support.

Albert rubbed his chin and nodded. "Yes, he should visit his family. With all this work, training, and school, you both deserve a little vacation."

"Okay," Cordelia sighed.

Her stomach twisted. After a long year, she was going to see her father again.

"When are we leaving?" Cordelia asked.

"Right away. We'll fly to Michigan on Friday. Saturday morning, I'll take you to see your dad."

"What about the Olympics tryouts?" Cordelia asked. "Tryouts are in one month and I'll miss a lot of practice. Should we go after tryouts?"

"No, I think this is more important," Albert replied. "I think it's the key to controlling your powers."

"Really?" she asked. A sliver of hope crept back into her heart.

"Yes," Albert said. "That's what my gut is telling me. Tell your professors and coach you'll be out of state for a few days."

"Okay, I'll let them know."

Albert dug into his pocket, pulled out an envelope, and said, "I took this out of my emergency fund. There's enough money for food, a hotel room, and a rental car. I'll buy plane tickets to Michigan."

Even though she was content with being in Florida, she couldn't wait to be home and see familiar places. Most of all, she missed Lake Michigan.

Traveling Circus and the Skeleton Key

13

Whitehall, Michigan

Sitting on the edge of the bed, Flynn stared at the large manila envelope with the Grand River Art and Music College logo on the front.

It's now or never, Flynn thought.

He ripped open the package, leafed through the paperwork, and read the letter.

Dear Flynn Parkes,

Thank you for your interest in our scholarship program and art competition. Per your request, I enclosed an application, rules, and regulations for this year's competition. The deadline for submission is October 17. All artwork must be delivered to Grand River Art and Music College no later than noon.

Winners will be announced at our school's open house on April 10. Dinner will be included in the application fee. Formal dress is required.

Good luck!

Sincerely,
   Professor Copley
   Grand River Art and Music College

Flynn's heart sank into his stomach. School already started and he had only a month to complete the project. He had a tight deadline with no time to waste.

With a heavy sigh, he stood and paced the floor. A stack of canvases, tubes of paint, and brushes sat unused. Flynn desperately searched his bedroom for inspiration.

He walked over to his bookshelf and thumbed through the art books. Skimming through the pages of a Van Gogh book, a flattened tulip with brown edges and a photograph fell to the floor. He picked it up and saw Rena sitting in front of a flower garden at the Tulip Time Festival. His mind drifted back to the school field trip. He remembered how her soft pink complexion was a stark contrast to a sea of purple flowers and her big brown eyes sparkled in the afternoon sun.

Snapping back to reality, Flynn looked down at the page it was bookmarking. The color plate was of a garden of blue irises with one lone white iris at the center.

Finally! I found my inspiration.

∽

Flynn heard rapid knock on his bedroom door.
"Come in!" Flynn said.
His dad popped his head into Flynn's bedroom. His rugged chin was unshaven and his hair was dotted with specks of sawdust.
"I just got home from work," Ray said. "Your mom and I wanted check on your progress."
"Sure," Flynn replied. "It's not ready yet, but you can come in."
"That's okay," Ray said as he entered the room. Georgia followed closely behind him.

Flynn dabbed his brush on the palette. His hands and clothes were covered in paint. Examining his painting of purple tulips in a garden, he plotted the last few strokes. He drew a long stem and then painted a white bud atop it. Satisfied, he stepped back, crossed his arms, and closed his eyes.

Don't become real, Flynn chanted over again.

"Oh no," Ray groaned.

Flynn's eyes snapped back open. A real white tulip blossomed out from the canvas right before everyone's eyes. In a clump of flowers, it became a lone tulip protruding from the canvas.

With narrowed eyes, Ray said, "You can't submit that piece. It will be cheating."

"Why not?" Flynn asked, narrowing his eyes. "I created it."

"It's unfair to use your special talent to win the competition," Ray replied. "You need to win the scholarship on your own merit."

"But I've tried everything else," Flynn protested. "And I still can't control my powers."

"You have a month before the deadline," Ray replied, crossing his arms. "You'll figure something out."

"I've been trying for a year! This isn't fair," Flynn stammered.

"Neither is cheating," Georgia replied.

Ray put his arm on Flynn's shoulder and said, "You can do it. I have faith in you."

Flynn grunted. Ray shook his head and marched out of the bedroom.

"The painting looks great," Georgia said.

"Thanks, Mom, I got the idea from the Tulip Festival," Flynn said, pointing to a photograph next to the painting. "I used Van Gogh's *Irises* painting as inspiration."

"Why did you paint a single white tulip in the middle of purple flowers?" Georgia asked.

"To me, it represents loneliness."

"Flynn, you're not alone," Georgia said with a furrowed brow and a sigh. "You'll create something for the competition. I know you can do it."

"I'll never control my powers."

Flynn glared at the painting he'd been so proud of only a few moments ago. He grabbed the wet canvas and carried it outside. His mom called after him, but he ignored her and tossed the painting in the trash can. Flynn jumped on his bike and took a long ride far away from the smell of oil paint, tulips, and the chastising looks of his parents.

I give up! Flynn felt his world collapse.

14

Whitehall High School, Michigan

The next morning at school, Flynn wandered over to Rena's locker. He wanted to tell her about what had happened the night before. As he rounded the corner in the hall, he saw her standing at her locker talking to Vinnie.

Vinnie was the exact opposite of Flynn; he looked and acted tough, and he had a muscular frame and brown hair slicked back with gel.

Why is she talking to him? Flynn bitterly thought.

They were laughing and smiling.

Grinding his teeth together, Flynn turned around and headed to his first class.

No matter how hard you try, you can't make someone like you, Flynn thought, staring off into space.

Halfway down the hall, Rena ran up beside him.

A bit out of breath, she asked, "Hey! What's wrong?"

Flynn stopped, turned, and looked into her eyes.

"My parents said I couldn't use my powers for the art scholarship," Flynn groaned, waving his empty hand in the air. "Now I have to start all over again from scratch."

"I'm sorry," she said, looking down at the floor.

"What's the deal with Vinnie?" Flynn asked.

Rena shrugged. "We're just friends."

After she had turned sixteen, Flynn hoped to take her out to the movies and get to know her outside of school.

"What were you guys talking about?" Flynn asked.

"I invited him to come see my band play the song for the competition. We're putting on a small concert for some friends. We'll be in the music room after school. You should come."

She invited Vinnie before me? Flynn thought. *What does she see in him?*

He mustered a smile. "Sure, I'll check it out."

Flynn felt like the last person invited to the party. He still had a crush on Rena and that was falling apart, too.

~

The final bell rang. Rena gathered her supplies and meandered over to Flynn's table.

"Hey, Flynn," Rena said. "Are you still coming?"

"Yeah, I just need to drop some stuff in my locker."

"Great," Rena said. "We need to setup, so you have time."

"See you then," Flynn said, giving her a wave.

Flynn slid out of the classroom and headed toward his locker.

Over his shoulder, he heard someone call out his name. He spun and saw Alden Nash sprinting down the hall.

Holding up the pocket watch, Alden came to abrupt stop a few feet away from Flynn.

"I brought it," Alden said, slightly out of breath.

Flynn stared at the watch that had given him so much trouble. The gold metal looked polished and free from any dents.

Alden popped open the lid. The glass cover was no longer cracked and the large hand on the clock ticked forward.

"It looks brand new," Flynn said.

"Yeah," Alden nodded. "Jaxon did a great job fixing it. Do you still want to buy it?"

"Yes," Flynn said.

"I think the watch is haunted," Alden said in hushed tone. "It was doing some crazy stuff when we were fixing it."

"Yeah, there's something strange about it," Flynn agreed.

Flynn reached into his back pocket for his wallet, counted out a hundred dollars, and then handed Alden the money.

"It's all yours," Alden said, handing Flynn the pocket watch. "Jaxon is waiting for me, so I'll talk to you later."

Flynn nodded and tucked the watch into his pants pocket.

~

Inside the music room, Vinnie was talking to Rena while she setup her drums. A boy Flynn didn't recognize tuned a guitar, and Sarah, a tall blonde girl from band class, stood at a microphone humming to herself.

Flynn hung in the back of the room, letting them get ready to perform. He waved and tried to get Rena's attention, but she was too busy talking to Vinnie to notice. Frustrated, Flynn sat down in the second row.

Then Ruben, Vinnie's best friend, showed up with a few football players. They all huddled around the band, talking loudly and high-fiving the guitar player.

Sarah pointed to the chairs, glared at the unruly boys, and said, "Sit down, we're ready to start."

"Oh look, It's Flynch," Ruben said as he pretended to punch Flynn's shoulder, only pulling back his fist at the last second.

Vinnie, Ruben and the football players burst into laughter and took their seats. Surrounded by muscular boys, Flynn wished he had the power to disappear. But then Rena spotted him and smiled.

Just ignore these guys for a little while, Flynn thought.

Then his thoughts turned to his painting and how he had thrown it out. He became agitated when his thoughts turned negative.

Once the band started, tuning out Vinnie and Ruben got easier. Sarah's voice started soft and wispy over a soft guitar line, but halfway through the first verse it picked up when Rena joined in, becoming a lively song that made Flynn's feet tap.

Great song, Flynn thought. *I hope she wins the scholarship.*

A few people stood and started dancing. Rena's face turned bright red and she sped up the tempo. The music came to abrupt end before more students joined in the dance.

Giving Rena a stern stare, Sarah asked, "What's the deal? Why did you rush the last chorus?"

"Sorry," Rena said, "I was trying something new."

"Just give me a heads-up next time," Sarah said.

"Okay, I will."

Flynn jumped out of his seat and hurried up to Rena before Vinnie could get in the way.

Rena set her drumsticks down, stretched her fingers, and asked, "What did you think?"

"It was awesome!" Flynn said. "I knew you could do it."

"Thanks, it was a lot of work. I think we're ready to record it now. I'll submit it next week so I'm not late."

Before Flynn could respond, the football team descended on the band. Flynn tried to make his escape, but instead he turned and bumped into Vinnie chest.

"Watch it, weirdo."

"Sorry."

Flynn stepped aside, but the other guys surrounded him. A bead of sweat formed on Flynn's brow.

I wish I could draw myself a hole and disappear, Flynn thought.

"Flynch," Ruben started to chant. The others joined in.

"Leave me alone. I said sorry." Flynn tried to back away again, but there were too many people around him.

"Leave him alone," Rena shouted.

Vinnie threw a fist. Flynn leaned to his side as Vinnie's fist grazed his cheek. Flynn wasn't sure if he was faking him out, but he was fed up with everyone, especially Vinnie. Before Flynn could raise his fists in defense, Vinnie took another swing. His fist slammed against Flynn's jaw, knocking him backward and causing him to see stars. With a sore chin, Flynn lost his balance and reached out to catch himself. Landing hands first on the floor, he heard a pop. Pain shot through his right wrist.

Feeling dizzy, Flynn sat on the floor and held his throbbing hand. Rena rushed to his side as the football players left the music room. Flynn tried to move his hand, but the pain was too intense.

Oh no! I think it's broken, Flynn speculated. *How am I going to draw now?*

15

Leviathan Prison, Siren Bay, Michigan

The barbed wire fence and barred windows looked like fangs. The concrete block walls cast a dark shadow over Cordelia and Albert. With each passing step toward the front entrance to the prison, she regretted asking Marcel to stay in the car.

A prison guard, dressed in a well-pressed uniform, was polite and professional as he greeted them in the lobby. Albert filled out paperwork and another guard led them to the visitation area. Cordelia felt like she was walking into the belly of a monster as her heels clicked on the tile floor.

Passing through a series of locked doors, the guard turned down a hall and opened a door to a large room. Men in blue shirts and pants sat at tables with family members. In hushed tones, the prisoners spoke with loved ones. Their conversations filled with regret and their desire to go home.

A guard sat nearby and the security cameras in all four corners spied on everyone.

How can they live under a microscope? Cordelia wondered.

She sat down on a cold metal chair and Albert sat down beside her.

The musty air in the room made her nose twitch. She fidgeted in her seat, trying to feel less awkward. The air conditioning pushed a cold breeze through the room and gave her goose bumps. She shivered, but her heart remained warm.

Avoiding eye contact with the prisoners, her gaze darted to the posters on the walls. One had a man walking down a beach. Under his footprints were the words, "Find peace with your past."

Cordelia sighed. The words sounded nice on paper.

A door on the opposite side of the room opened to reveal her dad being escorted by another guard. With slumped shoulders, Salvatore shuffled. His swollen eyes were filled with despair. He looked thinner than Cordelia had ever seen him.

"I'm so glad both of you came," Salvatore said with a weary smile.

Albert gave his son a stern look, leaned back in his chair, and crossed his arms.

Cordelia sat stiffly in the uncomfortable chair. "Hi, Dad."

"I wish I could give you a hug, but the guard said physical contact is against the rules," Salvatore said as he sat down across the table from them.

"I understand," Cordelia said.

"I kept calling and writing. I wanted to make sure you were okay, but you didn't answer. I needed to see you."

"And now, here I am," Cordelia said.

"How are things with you?" Salvatore asked.

Giving Albert a warm glance, Cordelia said, "Grandpa is taking good care of me. Marcel and I are both taking college classes part time and I'm training for the upcoming Olympic qualifiers."

"I'm so glad you haven't given up on your dream." Salvatore wiped a tear from his cheek. "You deserve a chance to compete. You really do."

It was the first time she'd seen him cry since her mother's funeral. Her shoulders relaxed a little.

"When do you leave?" Salvatore asked.

"Our flight leaves tomorrow night," Albert gruffly answered. "Cordelia has to get back for training."

Salvatore held his stomach and groaned.

Cordelia leaned forward. "Are you okay?"

"I haven't been eating a lot and I can't sleep at night," Salvatore said with a tear in his eye. "I have nightmares about being swallowed up by this dark prison. I feel like I'm drowning in here."

More tears? Crying twice in less than an hour? Cordelia thought.

"I've missed you," Salvatore said.

"I've missed the old you," she whispered.

He humbly stared at the table. "I'm sorry for the way I treated you and how I abandoned you. Everything changed after your mom died."

She leaned back in her seat. She was tired of his apologies and she wanted action rather than words.

"Can you ever forgive me?" Salvatore asked.

She curled her hands into fists and pondered his request.

"I'll try," she whispered.

"You've messed a lot of things up," Albert grumbled.

Salvatore's face lit up. "I'll find a way to make things right. I'll find a way to regain everyone's trust."

"I hope so," Albert said.

"The pocket watch brought out the worst in me." Salvatore looked at Cordelia. "It suppressed my sadness and I lost the ability to recognize pain in others. The dark side of human nature took over. But now that the watch has been destroyed, I feel like a weight has been lifted off my shoulders. I can feel compassion again."

Her dad's eyes were no longer charcoal, they were brown like they used to be. She couldn't deny that he was acting different, too.

Has my dad really changed? How will I know? she wondered.

Looking down at the floor, Cordelia crossed her arms. She wanted her burden to be lifted instead of being cursed by the spell.

"But now... I know I betrayed you, your grandfather, and everyone who worked for the circus. And all the people I tricked into giving me their money."

"That's why you're here," Albert said, placing his index finger on the table. "I'm glad you're realizing your mistakes."

Cordelia wanted to believe her dad's words.

Is my dad lying? Did the pocket watch bring out the worst in him? A small voice in the back of her head was skeptical.

"You hurt a lot of people," Cordelia said, fighting back tears. "Including me."

"I'm sorry." Salvatore looked earnest and concerned.

Albert sighed, "But why? Why did you steal from people?"

"Everything Jack said made so much sense," Salvatore said and turned to Albert. "Jack said I should take over the circus. I wanted to show you that I could run the circus better and make it more profitable. Prove to you that I'm not a failure."

Albert shook his head. "I wish you had chosen a different path."

Cordelia's cheeks reddened and her anger simmered.

"But what you did was wrong!" she stammered. "No wonder you never told Grandpa your true plans."

Salvatore fiddled with his fingers on the tabletop. "Do you know why I left you with the circus?"

Cordelia leaned forward and asked, "No, why?"

"I wanted to figure out how to save your mom from the car accident."

"But you said you couldn't control the watch when you travelled back in time?" Cordelia said.

"Yes," Salvatore nodded. "I can't control time completely."

My dad had trouble controlling his powers, too? Cordelia thought.

"Remember when I came back?" Salvatore asked. "I told you that I had a plan for bringing back your mom and breaking the mermaid curse?"

Her shoulders tightened and she whispered, "Yes."

"When I left the circus, Jack tracked me down because he wanted to make me a deal. If I gave him money and the scroll, then he would tell me how to save my wife."

"What?!" Cordelia narrowed her eyes.

Nearly jumping out of his seat, Albert asked, "How did Jack know about the scroll?"

"Jack is Viktor Rusalka's son-in-law," Salvatore said.

Cordelia's jaw dropped and her heart skipped a beat. She remembered the creepy old man with scraggly hair and yellow teeth. Viktor tried taking the scroll away from her family.

"Viktor had three kids, Rio, Murphy, and Shirley. Shirley is married to Jack."

"So Jack wanted the scroll back for his family," Cordelia started putting the pieces together in her head.

"Yes," Salvatore said. "Jack made me a deal. If I gave him $500,000 and the scroll, he would tell me how I could control my powers. Then I could bring your mom back. First we were going to steal from people and then rob banks."

My dad did all of this for love? Cordelia thought. The ice on her heart melted a little.

"So that's why you were stealing the money," Albert said bitterly. "To pay off Jack?"

"Yes," Salvatore said.

"How can you bring mom back?" Cordelia was confused.

"There's a second spell, one that allows you to control the power within yourself. Viktor found the scroll and a second spell a long time ago when he was in the war."

"But Viktor is dead," Cordelia said. "How can we find it now?"

"Jack knows where to find it," Salvatore said.

Cordelia looked up at her father. His face was pale with regret.

"I tried telling you sooner." Salvatore held out his hands. "I sent letters, but you never responded to my messages. I tried calling, but your grandpa never accepted my collect calls."

"Because we're still mad at you," Cordelia stammered with red cheeks, gritting her teeth.

"If you would've told us the truth from the beginning, maybe we could've figured everything out," Albert said.

"I know." Salvatore glanced up at Cordelia. "But there's more bad news."

"More?" Cordelia asked.

"Jack is here, in the same prison. Viktor's sons, Rio and Murphy, are in here, too."

Cordelia fidgeted in her seat. Images of Rio and Murphy flashed through her memory. She remembered being kidnapped and locked in a cabin bedroom with boarded windows while Rio and Murphy stood guard outside. And Viktor used the skeleton key to shoot lightning bolts at the police. All the old memories filled her with fear.

"Jack has the ledgers from the circus, and the employee

contracts. He had a whole plan written out," Salvatore said. "If you could find those documents, my lawyer might convince the judge that Jack was the real mastermind of the circus. The new evidence could reduce my sentence."

Cordelia took in the other people visiting in the room while she thought about her father's words.

"Really?" Cordelia asked.

"Yes," Salvatore said in a shaky voice. "I'm trying to find out where the second spell is located. I tried reaching out to Jack, but I think he's scheming with Rio and Murphy. They want the scroll. I can't protect you if I'm in prison, so be careful."

"Okay, Dad."

Albert put his hand on Cordelia's shoulder and gently squeezed.

The door on the opposite wall opened and the guards came to retrieve the prisoners. Visitation time was up and the visitors trickled out another door. Salvatore was the last one to be called.

Can I trust him again? Cordelia wondered.

She wanted her father home, but only if he was really changed. She wasn't ready to commit to anything yet.

"I'll talk it over with Cordelia," Albert said. "We'll figure it out."

"Thank you," Salvatore said.

A burly guard with a chiseled jaw tapped Salvatore on the shoulder and said, "Come on, your time is up."

Salvatore nodded and stood. Cordelia watched as the guard led her father away.

Suddenly, sirens began to screech followed by shouting, a loud bang, and growling. With guns drawn, the prison guards ran into the hall. The hairs on Cordelia's arms straightened and her fingers gripped the edge of her chair.

16

Cordelia's shoulders shivered and her knees shook.

"What's going on?!" she asked.

"I don't know," Salvatore said, shielding Cordelia from danger with his arm.

When no threat presented itself, Salvatore walked to the door and peeked around the corner. Cordelia and Albert followed closely behind and peered over his shoulder.

Two lions and a lioness chased three prison guards down the hall and cornered them inside an adjacent office space. With his back pressed up against the back wall, the burly guard took aim with his gun. A tall skinny officer with a large ring of keys jumped behind the door and the female guard hid underneath a desk.

With fear in his eyes, the skinny guard shouted, "Where did they come from?"

The burly guard reached down, pressed a button on his walkie-talkie, and yelled, "Visitation room needs back-up now!"

The lioness entered the office, jumped on top of the desk, and swiped all the papers onto the floor. The female guard screamed as papers rained down around her.

"What do we do now?" the woman shouted.

With claws out, the lion approached the skinny guard hiding behind the door and smacked the gun out of his hand. The lioness leapt off the desk and prowled around the office. Frightened, the skinny guard darted out of the room. The burly guard shot next to the lion's feet, trying to scare the beasts, but it only made them angrier.

Jack, Rio, and Murphy appeared down the hall. Cordelia almost didn't recognize Jack without his brown fedora. She didn't realize Jack had grey crew-cut hair under his hat. Rio's long thin legs lurched down the corridor. His shirt sleeves were rolled past his elbow exposing his tattoo-covered arms. Murphy's prison jumpsuit barely fit his stocky frame.

Jack pulled a mouse from a laundry bag, bent down, and set it on the floor. As he petted the tiny animal, it morphed and grew into another lion.

The beast barreled down the hall, knocking the skinny guard to the ground like a bowling pin. The lion jumped on top of the fallen man, pinned him to the floor, and roared inches from the guard's face. The sound echoed through the halls.

"Give me your keys!" Jack shouted.

The officer twisted and turned on the floor. His face was pale and eyes were wide. The officer frantically unlatched his keys from his belt and threw them to Jack.

Jack snapped his fingers and the lion backed away. Without his gun, the officer scurried down the hall. Jack unlocked the gates leading to the main entrance. His animals stood guard and waited for their trainer's command.

Jack handed the handcuffs to Rio and said, "We're going to need these."

Rio nodded and tucked the handcuffs in his prison jumpsuit pocket.

"Oh no," Cordelia gasped, adrenaline pumping through her veins. "They're escaping!"

Jack pointed to Cordelia and shouted, "There she is!"

Gritting his teeth, her dad slammed the door shut and wedged a chair underneath the handle. Grabbing her hand, he pulled her into the corner of the room. He flipped over a table. They ducked behind it and crouched down on the floor.

"I wish I had my pocket watch," Salvatore said with sweat dripping from his forehead.

"Me, too," Cordelia stammered.

"We need Marcel!" Albert said.

"He's waiting in the car outside," Cordelia said.

"I wonder if he heard the sirens?" Albert asked.

Before anyone could answer the question, a loud banging sounded on the door as though someone were kicking it. The chair flew across the floor and hit the wall. Loud footsteps tapped across the tiled floor.

Cordelia trembled as the noise grew louder.

"You can run, but you can't hide," Jack said, pushing the table aside.

Cordelia looked up. Jack towered over them.

Leaping to his feet, Salvatore ran shoulder-first into Jack and knocked him down. Cordelia watched in horror as her dad and Jack scuffled on the floor.

"Run, Cordelia!" her dad yelled.

With wobbly knees, Cordelia and Albert stood and ran toward the exit. Rio and Murphy walked through the door and blocked their path.

"You're not going anywhere!" Rio said.

Murphy grabbed Cordelia by the elbow and slapped the handcuffs on her wrists. Albert tried to intervene, but Rio tackled Albert to the ground.

Murphy dragged Cordelia out the door and into the hall. She tried pulling away, but his grip was too tight.

The lions had cornered the remaining guards in the hall while others laid on the floor with guns drawn. Murphy yanked Cordelia down the corridor and through the open gate. Cordelia kicked, screamed, and broke away from his grip. Murphy grabbed her by the waist and threw her over his shoulder. He carried her through the main entrance, out the front door, and down the sidewalk.

Murphy whistled and waved his hand in the air. Seconds later, a car pulled up to the curb in front of the building. Cordelia took a good look at the woman, who had greasy hair and a weathered face, but she didn't recognize her. She wore faded blue jeans and her arms were tan as though she worked outside. Murphy opened the back door, pushed Cordelia inside, and jumped into the seat beside her.

Rio ran out of the building, jumped in the back seat, and said, "Hey Shirley, we're sure glad to see you!"

Murphy leaned over the seat and gave the woman a hug.

"Sis," Murphy said. "Thanks for coming for us."

"Of course," Shirley said in gravelly voice. "I had to save my brothers and husband."

Brothers? Jack is her husband? Cordelia thought. *They're all related to Viktor? Dad was telling us the truth!*

"Yeah," Rio said. "I feel horrible we missed dad's funeral, stuck in prison and all. At least we got to see him in prison before he passed."

Shirley became teary eyed and said, "Dad should've never died in prison."

Hearing a ruckus outside, Cordelia turned her attention back to the chaos. All three lions and Jack ran out the front door of the prison.

Looking out the back window, Cordelia saw Marcel jump out of the rental car and yell, "Stop!"

"Who's that guy?" Murphy asked. "Jack better hurry up, we got trouble. I'm not going back to jail."

"We're not leaving without my husband," Shirley said.

Noticing Marcel, Jack whistled and pointed toward the rental car. On command, the lions snapped to attention and charged through the parking lot.

Marcel backed away from the car as the lions approached. One jumped on the hood, creating a huge dent. The lioness smashed the grill and headlights with her paws. And the other lions punctured the front tires with their fangs.

POP!

The tire went flat. Cordelia's heart sank.

Jack snapped his fingers. On command, the lions stopped, turned around, and ran back to their trainer's side.

Pulling out his dumbbells from the trunk, Marcel frantically curled the weights until his muscles were the size of tree trunks and he stood nearly twelve feet tall.

Jack reached down and petted the lions. One by one they morphed back into mice. He scooped them up and placed them into his laundry bag. The guards spilled out of the jail. Jack jumped into the passenger seat of the getaway car and slammed the door shut. Shirley gripped the steering wheel and the car tore through the parking lot.

Marcel chased behind them on foot. With lightning speed, Marcel caught up to the car and grabbed onto the bumper with his good arm. The car swerved, tires squealed, and smoke rolled from the wheel wells as Marcel dug his heels into the pavement. The smell of burnt rubber filled the air.

Metal crunched and the bumper snapped off. Marcel fell backwards and tumbled to the ground. The car skidded across the parking lot and smashed into a few parked cars. Shirley regained control of the steering wheel, punched the gas pedal, and the car lurched forward. Cordelia's back slammed against the seat as the car sped out of the parking lot.

17

Crammed between Rio and Murphy, Cordelia couldn't reach the car door handles. Her worry turned to fear when she imagined the worst outcome.

"Let me go!" Cordelia shouted from the back seat.

"No," Jack yelled. "We need you."

"Where are you taking me?"

Rio turned to Cordelia and demanded, "Where's the skeleton key and scroll?"

Cordelia gritted her teeth, unwilling to give them any details. Murphy twisted her arm.

"Ouch!" Cordelia cried.

Pointing a crooked finger in her face, Rio demanded, "Tell me! Or Jack will sic the lions on you."

Jack held up a mouse and jabbed it in her face. Cordelia squirmed in her seat, turned, and looked away. Rio gripped her arm, making her whimper in pain.

"My grandpa put it in the safety deposit box," Cordelia blurted out, wishing the pain would stop.

"Where?" Jack grunted.

She reluctantly gave them the name and address of the bank.

"Let's go get it," Rio said. "First, we need to ditch this car. The police will be looking for it."

"We got it covered, thanks to my wife," Jack said and then smiled at Shirley.

What are they going to do with me after they get the scroll? Cordelia worried.

～

Cordelia watched trees, cornfields, and farm houses whiz by the car window as they drove for what seemed like forever. Heading west toward Lake Michigan, the towns started to look familiar.

Jack leaned forward and kissed Shirley on the cheek. "Thanks, honey, for doing this."

"I missed you!" Shirley said.

"Missed you, too," Jack said, holding his wife's hand.

Cordelia wanted answers to the million questions running through her head.

"How did you know I was going to visit my dad?" Cordelia asked.

"A prison guard told me Salvatore was going to have visitors today," Jack said. "I knew it had to be you. No one else would come visit him."

"How did you guys escape?" Shirley asked.

"I lured mice into my cell with bread crumbs and then I trained them at night," Jack said. "When the doors opened for our outdoor recreation time, I snuck into the hallway with the mice and changed them into lions. Then I unleashed them on the guards. It was total chaos. The guards didn't have a chance. I slipped away, cornered a guard, and stole his keys. Then I set Rio and Murphy free."

"Thanks, Jack." Rio said.

Murphy nodded. "I'm glad to be outta there."

"You're all crazy!" Cordelia blurted out.

Noticing a rest area sign, Shirley said, "The second getaway car is at this rest stop. I brought new clothes for everyone to change into. The suitcase is in the trunk."

When they pulled into the empty parking lot, Cordelia wondered *Maybe I can run away? I'll call the police if there's a payphone inside. Or maybe I should yell for help?*

Cordelia didn't see any cars or people walking around. There were a few semi-trucks with their engines idling.

"I need to use the bathroom," Cordelia said.

Rio grabbed Cordelia's arm. "Not so fast."

Looking at his wife, Jack said, "Can you keep an eye on her?"

Shirley nodded. The doors unlocked and Murphy opened it with one hand while holding onto Cordelia's arm with the other. She patiently waited for her opportunity to escape.

Shirley popped the trunk of the getaway car and grabbed the suitcase.

Jack reached into his bag, pulled out one of the mice, and dropped it into his shirt pocket.

"Don't get any ideas, Cordelia," Jack said. "Lions can outrun humans."

Cordelia frowned and narrowed her eyes. Rio draped his coat over her hands, covering the handcuffs around her wrists. As the five of them walked into the rest center, Cordelia heard some loose change jingling in her pocket.

Where's the payphone? she thought.

Inside the building, Cordelia surveyed the room filled with vending machines and a brochure rack. She eyed the payphone hanging on the wall outside the bathroom entrance. Shirley followed Cordelia into the bathroom. Shirley unlocked the handcuffs and stood guard while Cordelia went inside the stall.

Cordelia remerged a few minutes later and took her time washing her hands, hoping all the running water would urge Shirley to have to go too.

"Wait here. I'll be right back," Shirley said.

Shirley slapped the handcuffs back on Cordelia's wrists and ducked into a stall.

Yes! Cordelia grinned. *My plan worked!*

Cordelia darted out of the bathroom. She struggled to reach inside her pocket to find a quarter. Her hands trembled and her knees shook as she reached for the payphone. A cold hand clamped down on her shoulder and pulled Cordelia away from the phone.

"I knew you'd try something," Murphy grunted. "Luckily Jack didn't see you."

With scowls on their faces, Jack, Rio, and Shirley joined them a minute later. The men had changed into the newly pressed clothes.

"Trying to sneak away?" Shirley snarled.

Cordelia's throat turned dry and she took a gulp of air.

Murphy pushed Cordelia outside, stopping in front of a giant map of Michigan on the front wall of the building. A red star placed them near Shelby.

Pointing to a rusted four-door car, Shirley said, "I have the other car here, just like you asked."

"Good job," Jack said, rubbing his wife's shoulder. "I'll drive from here."

~

The bank had polished windows and neatly trimmed hedges and trees. Jack parked the car toward the back of the lot, far away from the customers. Cordelia looked down at the handcuffs, wishing she could break free.

"Did you bring it?" Jack asked Shirley.

Nodding, she reached under the seat, pulled out a box, and handed it to Jack. He opened the box and pulled out a handgun.

"Be careful, I don't want to lose you again," Shirley said.

"I will." Jack said. He then turned around in his seat and glared at Cordelia. "I don't want any fuss out of you."

Cordelia nodded, even though she was mulling over her escape options.

"Rio is going to unlock your cuffs, but don't try running away," Jack said, tucking the pistol into his coat pocket.

Cordelia's arms trembled as Rio unlocked the cuffs.

"I'll do all the talking," Jack said. "The rest of you, wait here."

He got out of the car, opened the back door, and let out Cordelia.

A tingling sensation ran through Cordelia's arms. She rubbed her sore wrists and walked toward the bank with Jack prodding her along. Jack opened the front door and nervously looked around the empty lobby.

Traveling Circus and the Skeleton Key

No security guards?! Cordelia thought. *Should I scream? What will Jack do with the gun?*

Jack nudged Cordelia toward the counter. She stepped up to a middle-aged bank teller with curly hair.

"Hello," the smiling lady behind the counter said. "How can I help you?"

Cordelia was too nervous to speak.

"We're here to check on a safety deposit box," Jack replied.

"Okay, I'll need to see some ID and I need to compare your signature with the one on file," the lady said and handing them paperwork to sign and fill out.

Cordelia handed the lady her license and filled out the paperwork.

The bank teller compared the signature and nodded. She typed on her computer and looked up the information.

"Here it is, box number seven," the bank teller said. "Follow me."

Jack and Cordelia started to follow the lady.

The bank teller turned to Jack and asked, "Are you on the list? I'll need to see your ID too."

Jack narrowed his eyes and scowled at Cordelia.

"No," Jack grunted.

"Sorry," the bank teller politely replied. "We only let people registered to the box enter the back room. I apologize for the inconvenience. Bank rules."

Jack shook his head and muttered, "Okay."

He tapped his fingers on the front counter and waited.

The lady led Cordelia to the back of the bank. They walked down a short narrow hallway and turned into a small room. A row of metal boxes with numbers on them lined the back wall.

"Here you go," the bank teller said, handing Cordelia a key. "When you're done, bring the key back to the lobby."

Cordelia held up both hands. Her fingers trembled.

"Wait," Cordelia whispered. "That guy outside just escaped prison. He brought me here against my will."

The lady stumbled backward and her eyes widened.

"I knew something wasn't right," the bank teller talked in hushed tones. "Stay here, I'll call the police."

The lady cautiously left Cordelia alone in the room. Cordelia slid behind the door and pressed her back against the wall. Using the breathing techniques she learned from her coach, she tried slowing down her pounding heart.

A few moments later, Jack yelled, "What's taking so long!?"

Cordelia heard a scuffling sound and then loud footsteps. Cordelia looked up at the ceiling and started breathing rapidly.

Jack burst into the room. He had his gun pressed against the bank teller's ribs. He spun around and saw Cordelia hiding behind the door. Cordelia whimpered and the bank teller started crying.

Jack snatched the key out of Cordelia's hand and raced over to the boxes. His eyes scanned the numbers and his face lit up. He opened the box and reached inside. With an evil laugh, he held up the Secret Talent Scroll and the skeleton key.

18

Jack dragged Cordelia by the elbow out of the bank and down the sidewalk to the car. Jack tossed the skeleton key to Rio. Murphy, who was leaning against the car, slapped the handcuffs onto Cordelia's wrists and shoved her into the back seat.

"Excellent!" Rio said. "Did you get the scroll, too?"

Jack nodded.

"Good," Rio said with a sly smile. "Now, I can follow in Dad's footsteps and control the power of lightning."

Oh no! Cordelia worried. *I can't let that happen.*

"Help me!" Cordelia screamed and kicked the floor boards.

Murphy covered her mouth with his sweaty hand and grunted, "Quiet!"

Cordelia squirmed in the seat, but Murphy leaned into her body with his rugged elbow and squished her into the seat cushions. The musty smell from the prison lingered in the air.

Cordelia heard the faint sound of sirens in the distance.

"I hear the cops!" Shirley said. "Let's get out of here!"

"Hold on," Jack said. "I have an idea."

Jack unrolled the scroll on the front seat of the car and read the chant. A gust of wind kicked up sand from the pavement and blew it into the open car window. Jack reached into his pants pocket, pulled out a lighter, and flicked the flint wheel with his thumb. The sand passed through the flame and ignited it into a tiny firework show. Murphy removed his hand from Cordelia's mouth and watched in awe as the cap on Shirley's water bottle popped off. Water shot from the bottle and extinguished the sparks. The ash fluttered onto the skeleton key.

Rio shivered. "I feel the electricity flowing through the key!"

Cordelia's eyes widened and her body trembled.

Oh no! she worried.

"You got what you wanted, now let me go!" Cordelia grabbed the door handle but it was locked.

"Not so fast," Jack said. "We still need you!"

"For what?" Cordelia stammered.

"There's a ribbon that was wrapped around the scroll when my dad found it long ago," Rio said. "The ribbon is locked inside my dad's suitcase buried on the L.C. Woodruff ship near the White Lake Pier. There's a third spell written on the ribbon that lets you control the power within yourself. And the skeleton key opens the suitcase."

"After you turn into a mermaid tonight, you're going to find the ribbon," Jack added.

Cordelia's stomach churned. Her nightmare wasn't over.

Police sirens echoed through the air and grew louder.

"They're coming for us!" Shirley shouted with a worried look.

With lights flashing, four cop cars barreled into the bank parking lot, screeched to halt, and formed a circle around the car.

They're here to save me! Cordelia thought. Her fingernails dug into the seat cushion.

With guns drawn, the cops jumped out of their cars and took cover behind the doors.

Shirley slid down in her seat and covered her head.

A commanding officer spoke into a bullhorn. "Come out with your hands up!"

"I'll take care of them!" Jack grunted and opened the laundry bag.

"No," Rio shook his head. "I got this."

Rio rolled down the window and pointed the key at the cop cars. A lightning bolt flew from the tip of key and struck one of the cars. The officers ducked for cover and landed heavily on the asphalt.

The officers shouted back and forth as they ran from their vehicles.

Another lightning bolt shot from the key and struck a second car. The tires exploded and the windshield shattered. Fragments of glass sprayed all over the parking lot.

Cordelia's body trembled. She hunched low in her seat and peered out the window.

Another bolt arced in the air and struck the back half of the other two cars.

BANG!

The cars burst into flames and black smoke billowed from underneath the hoods.

Laughing, Rio lowered the key. "Good luck chasing us now."

Jack started the car, punched the gas pedal, and broke through the line of destroyed cars. Cordelia leaned sideways as they veered onto the main street and sped away.

A car whizzed by her window and Cordelia caught a glimpse of her grandpa and Marcel driving in the direction of the bank. She tried waving out the side window, but they were already gone. Rio grabbed her arms and pushed her back into the seat.

19

The wood frame around the oil painting was smashed and a rip ran through the center of the canvas. The artwork barely fit in the metal trash can. All Flynn's hard work over the past year was for nothing and he wouldn't qualify for the art competition.

Flynn doused his painting with gasoline and lit a match.

POOF!

Cursing his powers, he watched his dreams of becoming an artist go up in smoke. The single white tulip shriveled on the stem and the oil pigment blistered orange. Purple smoke billowed from the fire. Slowly, the wood frame turned to blackened ash and crumbled to the bottom of the trash can. When the painting turned into a heap of glowing embers, Flynn soaked the remaining ashes with water from a garden hose. Steam chased away the purple smoke.

Fighting back tears, he stared into the trash can and thought about all the events that had led to this day. His trance was broken by the sound of the phone ringing inside the house. He tossed the hose aside and hurried to answer it.

"Hello."

"Hey Flynn, it's Rena."

"Hi, Rena." His spirit lifted a little. "Happy sixteenth birthday."

"Thanks. I called because I wanted to tell you I'm sorry for what happened at school," Rena said with a hint of sympathy in her voice.

Looking down at his hand, Flynn winced in pain. The doctor

had prescribed a compression wrist brace and painkillers to treat his sprain.

"It's not your fault," Flynn said.

"I know, but I never should've invited Vinnie to my concert," Rena said. "It was my mistake."

Flynn remained silent, absorbing her apology.

"I know this is short notice, but I was wondering if you wanted to go to the movies tonight?"

Does she like me or feel sorry for me? Flynn wondered.

"Come on," Rena prodded him. "It'll be fun to hang out together by ourselves."

Would this be a real date? he thought.

"Just the two of us?" Flynn asked, feeling a bit more interested.

"Yes," Rena said enthusiastically.

"Okay, I'll go, but I need to ask my parents. They're at work right now, but. I'm sure they'll say yes. I'll need to be home by 11, though."

"No problem," Rena said. "My curfew is 11 pm, too. I'll stop by around six?"

"That works."

"Well, see you tonight," Rena said.

"Okay, I'll talk to you later. Bye."

Feeling upbeat, Flynn hung up the phone. He had waited a long time for this day even though he was embarrassed because he didn't have a car to pick her up.

Finally, a date with Rena, Flynn thought.

A rapid knock sounded on the front door.

Who's that? Flynn wondered.

He walked into the foyer and opened the door. Stumbling backward, Flynn's jaw dropped when he saw Albert and Marcel on the front porch. Albert, with tangled hair and red cheeks, stopped pacing mid-step. Bandages covered Marcel's right arm and hand.

Anxiety crept into Flynn's mind as he remembered all he had gone through at the hands of Marcel.

Marcel's shoulders slumped and his brow furrowed. "We could really use your help."

Traveling Circus and the Skeleton Key

"Cordelia is in trouble," Albert blurted out.

A purple orb the size of a golf ball hovered over Albert's right shoulder.

"Albert!" Flynn replied. "Where have you been?"

"It's a long story," Albert groaned. "Can you help us?"

"I don't know if I can help, I hurt my hand," Flynn said, showing them the compression wrist brace.

The purple orb whizzed past Flynn's ear and entered his home.

"What is that?" Flynn asked, pointing at the orb.

"The smoke from the crystal ball escaped," Albert replied. "It led me to your doorstep."

"Really?" Flynn asked.

Maybe Albert could fix my problems, Flynn thought anxiously. *But... it looks like he has his own problems.*

"Come inside," Flynn said. "A lot has happened in one year."

"Yes, indeed," Albert said. "Tell me about it."

One year ago, Flynn would've shut the door and hid inside the closet, but Albert had helped him find his courage through art. Flynn gestured toward the living room and welcomed them in. Albert and Marcel sat down on the couch.

"I wondered what happened to everyone," Flynn said. "You disappeared and you never came back to Funnell Field."

"Yes, the local newspaper wrote an article about Salvatore and the money he stole," Albert said. His eyes were filled with sorrow. "Our reputation was ruined. So, we moved the circus to Florida."

"I'm glad you're here. I need your help, too," Flynn said. "I can't control my powers."

"Hm, the scroll's powers seemed to be more unstable with younger people," Albert said. "Marcel and Cordelia struggle, too, but I think we found a solution to controlling your powers."

"Great!" Flynn said, feeling a sense of hope.

Looking agitated, Marcel sat on the edge of the couch with one knee bouncing out of control.

"What happened to Cordelia?" Flynn asked.

"Cordelia was kidnapped this morning," Marcel blurted out.

"Kidnapped?" Flynn's pulse raced. "Who did it? Why?"

"A man by the name of Viktor Rusalka lost the Secret Talent Scroll a long time ago," Albert said. "After Cordelia found the scroll, Viktor tried stealing it back. Viktor went to prison and died, but his sons, Rio and Murphy, joined forces with their brother in-law, Jack. Remember Jack?"

"He had the trained lions?" Flynn asked.

"Yep," Albert replied.

"And now they have Cordelia," Marcel said.

"What do they want from her?" Flynn asked.

"They want the scroll back. But now that they've got it, they must need something else," Albert said, wringing his hands.

"I'm not sure what I can do, but I owe you a lot," Flynn said. "You saved me from going to juvie."

"You're a good kid," Albert said. "You deserve a bright future."

Marcel cleared his throat. "Hey. Sorry about what I did to you. I'm trying not to be a jerk."

Flynn relaxed, *Maybe Marcel wasn't so bad after all.*

"What's the plan?" Flynn asked.

"I'm working out the details in my head, but first I need to build a team," Albert said.

"What about Sammy and Buster?" Flynn asked. "Can they help, too?"

"This morning, after Jack broke out of prison, I called them," Albert said. "I bought them plane tickets. Paula and Rego are coming, too. I hope they get here soon. We're running out of time."

"How are we going to find Cordelia?" Flynn asked, rocking back and forth.

"The ball was destroyed, but the smoke escaped and went into my lungs," Albert said. "I can feel it living inside me."

"Wow!" Flynn leaned back in a state of shock.

Pointing to the purple orb hovering over his shoulder, Albert said, "Someone was guiding us today."

"Really?" Flynn asked in shock.

"It led us to the bank where the scroll and key were kept inside a safety deposit box," Albert said. "Jack needed Cordelia's ID and her signature to get the scroll."

"But by the time we got to the bank, it was too late," Marcel said.

Albert nodded. "Rio has the ability to control lightning now, just like his father. He destroyed the police cars and they escaped, taking Cordelia with them."

"Where are they now?" Flynn asked.

"The smoke from the crystal ball gave me a vision of my wife, Elsa," Albert said. "In my vision, Elsa said Cordelia was trapped in a car with Jack and they were heading to the White Lake Pier. That's why we came back to Whitehall. And then she led us to your doorstep."

Flynn let out a long breath of air, digesting all the information.

"Why would they take her to the pier?" Flynn asked.

"If I had to make a guess," Albert said. "Jack wants her to find something on the sunken ship."

"Sunken ship?" Flynn asked, thoroughly confused.

Marcel chuckled, "Another long story." Looking at Albert, Marcel asked, "Now what do we do?"

"I'll call the car rental place and ask for a new vehicle. We barely made it here, the radiator started leaking anti-freeze. I'll call the police and let them know where to find us. Hopefully, by then, Paula, Rego, Sammy, and Buster will be here."

A knot formed in Flynn's stomach. Even though he had started taking bold actions, he felt his old insecurities creep into his mind.

"Can we stay here until the new rental car arrives?" Albert asked.

"Of course," Flynn said. "As long as you're gone before my parents get home. They would freak out."

"I understand," Albert said.

"What do you want me to do?" Flynn asked.

"I need a paper and a pencil," Albert said.

Flynn pointed to the pad of paper and pencil by the phone that his mother used for taking messages.

"Warm up your fingers!" Albert said. "I'll write a list of things I need you to draw. Tools we need to get Cordelia back. Using your powers, you can make the drawings real."

Albert scrawled out his list and handed Flynn the notepad. "Can you meet us at the White Lake Pier tonight before sunset?"

"Yes, Rena can give me a ride. We already had plans tonight."

There goes the movie, Flynn sighed. *But this will be more exciting!*

"It'll be dangerous," Albert cautioned.

"I think she'll be up for the adventure," Flynn said.

Albert gave him a weary smile.

Flynn gathered his art supplies from his room and started drawing on the kitchen table while Albert made more phone calls.

Squeezing his eyes shut, Flynn winced in pain as he adjusted the compression wrist brace. He popped an aspirin into his mouth and chased it with a glass of water. The painkillers helped, but he could only do short drawing stints before his hand began to throb.

Two hours later, when the new rental car arrived, Albert and Marcel left to get something to eat. Flynn checked the clock. He had a few hours left before his parents came home. Pushing through the agony, he flipped to a new sheet of paper and started sketching the last few things on Albert's list.

How are we going to pull this off? Flynn wondered, rubbing his sore wrist.

20

Cordelia stared out the car window. A lighthouse appeared above the tree line as Jack drove the car down a narrow road and pulled into the L.C. Woodruff Inn parking lot near the White Lake channel. He parked the car next to a U-Haul truck and shut off the engine.

An elderly woman with short gray hair stood next to the truck. The cool wind grew stronger and she put on a hand-knitted sweater.

She looks familiar, Cordelia thought. *Where have I seen her before?*

Rio and Murphy jumped out of the car and took turns hugging the old lady.

"My boys are free," the old woman exclaimed. "I'm so happy to see you."

"Mom," Rio said, acting tough. "That prison couldn't hold us."

That's Viktor's wife! Cordelia finally recognized the old woman. *Now I remember, she checked us into the Inn two years ago.*

Jack turned to Shirley and held her hand. "You and Murphy take the U-Haul truck and go home. Burn the evidence from my time at the circus while Murphy loads up all our stuff. When we're done here, your mom can drive us to the farm house."

"I arranged a freighter ship to take us back to Russia," Mrs. Rusalka said. "The captain wants exotic pets. Jack can make some animals in exchange for the boat ride."

"Yes," Jack said. "With the ribbon, I'll be able to change them into any animal I want!"

"And we can start a new life in Russia," Murphy added.

Turning to Shirley, Jack said, "If the police show up, leave without us."

"But I want to stay with you!" Shirley pleaded.

"It's too dangerous. Stick with the plan," Jack said. "Go home and burn any evidence. Use the money we saved and leave with all our stuff."

"I don't want to go without you," Shirley said.

"If we get captured, I don't want you to go to jail, too," Jack said.

Biting her lip, Shirley crossed her arms and leaned against the U-Haul.

"Mom, wait inside the Inn," Rio said. "When we're done, we'll come get you."

"Okay," Mrs. Rusalka replied.

Looking at Jack, Rio asked, "What do we do now?"

"We'll go down to the beach and wait for sunset." Jack grabbed Cordelia's arm and pulled her along. "We need a mermaid."

～

6 pm

Knock, Knock!

The bedroom door creaked open and Flynn's mom popped her head into his bedroom.

"Rena is here to pick you up," Georgia said.

"Okay, Mom."

As she closed the door, she said, "Don't forget curfew."

"Yes, Mom."

Flynn packed a large roll of drawing paper and several pencils into his backpack. He went downstairs and saw Rena in the living room, sitting on the couch. She smiled as he came into the room.

Flynn's dad stood up from his recliner chair and said, "Flynn, could I see you in the kitchen for a minute?"

Flynn's stomach grumbled.

Oh no! He knows something is up, Flynn thought. *He won't let me go.*

"Yeah, Dad?" Flynn replied, trying to act natural.

Flynn followed his dad into the kitchen and they stood next to the refrigerator. With his hands on his hips, Ray stared firmly into Flynn's eyes.

"Is everything okay?" Flynn asked nervously.

"Yeah," Ray whispered. "I wanted to make sure you had enough money to take Rena out and have a good time. I want you to be a gentleman and pay."

Flynn let out a sigh of relief and said, "Oh, I thought you were going tell me I couldn't go."

"No," Ray replied with a smirk. "I'm just glad you're no longer afraid to talk to girls."

"Gee, thanks, Dad," Flynn said.

Ray ruffled his son's hair and chuckled.

"It's okay," Flynn responded. "I have enough."

Ray tucked a twenty dollar bill into Flynn's shirt pocket and said, "Here's an extra 20, just in case. Have fun."

"Thanks, Dad."

They stepped back into the living room where his mother and Rena were talking.

Georgia stood, kissed Flynn's forehead, and said, "Have fun!"

Flynn nodded.

"The movie is at seven. Are you ready to go?" Rena asked.

"Yep," Flynn said.

As Flynn and Rena walked out the front door and down the sidewalk to the driveway, his parents stood in the doorway and waved goodbye.

Flynn dropped his backpack in the back seat and hopped into Rena's car.

"Do you want you to grab a bite to eat before the movie?" Rena asked as she started the engine. "We could pick up some fast food and take it to the marina."

"Hold on," Flynn said as he waited for his parents to walk back into the house. When they were gone, he said, "Pop the trunk. I need something out of the garage."

Traveling Circus and the Skeleton Key

With a puzzled look, Rena turned off the car and replied, "Okay…"

Flynn hopped out and ducked inside the garage. Before his parents came home he had hidden all the tools from Albert's list underneath a drop cloth. One by one he loaded the supplies into Rena's car. He saw her watching him in the side mirror. She was squinting and her lips were drawn tight. When he was done, he slid back into the car.

"What's going on?" Rena asked, crossing her arms.

"Ummm," Flynn stuttered and stared out the window. He wasn't sure how he was going to break the news. "The traveling circus came back to town."

"What!?" she exclaimed. "Did they all come back to Funnell Field?"

"No," Flynn said. "Not all the circus performers."

"Why didn't you tell me?"

"I didn't have a lot of time to call you. Albert and Marcel showed up at my house, asking for help. And then my parents came home from work."

She gave him a curious look. "What kind of help do they need?"

"This is where the story gets crazy."

"Crazy? Again?" Rena shook her head and smirked. "Seems like a pattern."

"Yeah, I know, but Cordelia is in trouble and Albert needs our help."

Letting out a long sigh, Rena uncrossed her arms and gripped the steering wheel.

"Albert said he might've found a way to help us control our powers," Flynn added.

Rena's face lit up. "That would be great."

Flynn nodded.

"I hope we're not late getting home," Rena said. She started the car and backed out of the driveway. "My parents will never let me see you again."

Flynn rubbed his forehead. "You're right. We're always getting into trouble together."

They laughed nervously.

If it took trouble, a fight at school or rescuing Cordelia, to get him time alone with Rena, he didn't mind one bit. He hoped their adventure would bring them closer together without getting hurt.

"Where are we going?" Rena asked, her eyes focused on the road.

"We're meeting them at the White Lake Pier before sunset. I brought my art supplies just in case I need to make more drawings."

"I wondered why you needed all that stuff."

She drove west toward Lake Michigan while Flynn explained the game plan.

~

Rena's car rumbled along a deserted gravel road, bouncing up and down with each pothole.

Albert and Marcel were leaning against the new rental car. Rena parked her car behind them.

"Do you have a backpack, too?" Flynn asked Rena. "We're going to need another bag to carry our supplies that I've drawn."

She nodded. "It's in the back seat."

They grabbed their backpacks and hopped out of the car to greet Albert and Marcel. Everyone was cordial, but somber due to the stressful situation.

"Are the others on their way?" Flynn asked. "Where are the police?"

Albert glanced up at the sun sinking in the sky. "They were supposed to be here by now."

"They should've been here a half hour ago," Marcel said, clenching and unclenching his fists.

"Are we heading to the beach?" Rena asked.

"We'll wait a little longer," Albert said. "If Paula and Rego use their wings, they can carry Sammy and Buster. I hope their flight isn't delayed and they get here before sunset."

Marcel checked his watch. "Almost sunset. How far away is the pier?"

"It's about a 30-minute walk," Flynn said. He looked at Marcel's bandaged arm and pointed. "You never told me what happened."

"A hurricane and sailboat a few days ago," Marcel responded.

"Hurricane! Sailboat?!" Rena's eyes widened. "Wow!"

"Yeah, it's healing pretty good. But I only have one good arm." Marcel made a fist and flexed his muscles.

"While we wait, Marcel can unpack his weights." Albert said. "And Flynn, where are the tools we need?"

"I have them in the trunk of Rena's car," Flynn said. "I'll go get them."

Albert nodded.

Rena popped the trunk and helped Flynn unload two large nets, a pair of binoculars, a flare gun, rope, and a few flashlights. Flynn and Rena gathered the equipment and stuffed them into their backpacks.

"Can you think of anything else we might need?" Rena asked.

"I have a drawing pad just in case. I didn't want to weigh us down with stuff."

Marcel rummaged through the trunk of the rental car and pulled out his gym bag containing his dumbbells.

"We'll find a hiding spot up in the dunes and wait for them to arrive with Cordelia," Albert said. Rubbing his forehead, he checked his watch again. "Where are Paula and Rego?"

"Hopefully they'll get here soon," said Marcel. "Otherwise we'll do this alone."

Flynn's shoulders tensed and he bit his bottom lip.

"Who knows what Jack has up his sleeve," Albert grumbled. "We need all the help we can get."

Flynn had a sinking feeling in his chest. He remembered being chased up a tree and almost eaten by Jack's lions.

"Are you sure you want to help us?" Flynn asked Rena "You can stay here and watch the cars."

Looking determined, she said, "No, I'll stay by your side."

The sun traveled toward the horizon. They waited patiently.

After what seemed like an hour, Albert finally said "We can't wait any longer for them. Hopefully, they'll find us on the beach.

We need to go."

The others nodded nervously in agreement.

They trekked down the road a few yards and then they veered off the gravel road and onto a hiking trail. Cutting through the ditch, they trudged down the worn path. The trail weaved through trees, bushes, and over hills. The solid soil changed into loose beach sand and the air turned cooler near the lake. They struggled up a sand dune, but when they reached the top, they looked out over Lake Michigan. To the north, waves lapped along the White Lake Channel and boardwalk. From the west, the wind swept over Lake Michigan, the beach, and the dunes.

"This looks like a good place to hide," Albert said, pointing to a group of trees around the lighthouse.

Flynn raised his binoculars to his eyes and scanned the beach. Most of the tourists had gone home for the day. A few beachgoers gathered up their towels, and meandered to their cars.

Pointing to the White Lake pier, Flynn said, "I see them over there."

As the sun sank below the horizon, Flynn saw Cordelia standing on the pier with two men.

"What do we do now?" Marcel asked.

"Wait for the police, Paula, and Rego to show up," Albert said.

Marcel crossed his arms and tapped his foot.

Flynn worried that the night might turn into chaos.

21

The horizon blushed from dusky pink to scarlet. All the different hues bounced off the lake and lit up the billowing clouds. The wind whipped Cordelia's red hair against her face and her heartbeat fell into the rhythm of the waves pounding against the White Lake Pier.

Can I find the ship again? she wondered.

Rio removed the coat draped over Cordelia's wrist and unlocked the handcuffs. Blood flowed faster through her arms and her hands tingled.

"Don't even try swimming away," Rio grunted, gripping her elbows.

Cordelia shook her head.

"I hope the current didn't bury the ship," Jack said.

"Yeah," Rio said. "Me too."

Jack held up an underwater metal detector and shovel, bundled together with rope.

"Here," Jack said, handing Cordelia the tools. "You're going to need them."

Cordelia grabbed the bundle and slung them over her shoulder.

"How will I know which luggage to grab?" Cordelia asked. "There could be hundreds of bags on the ship."

"Viktor's name is engraved on it," Rio replied.

"It's time," Jack said.

As the sun dipped below the horizon, Cordelia took a deep

breath and dove into Lake Michigan. Her fingers breached the water's surface and her legs fused together, turning into a long mermaid tail. Hidden in the dark water, she floated and pondered her next move.

Should I swim away or find the ribbon? Cordelia thought. *The ribbon is my only chance of competing in the Olympics, but if I could escape right now...*

Determined, she made up her mind, *I'll get the ribbon and then escape!*

Swishing her tail, she swam back in the direction where she had found the L.C. Woodruff two years ago. Holding the metal detector in her hand, she skimmed up and down the coast line. Making clicking sounds with her tongue, the sound waves bounced off any objects that were in her way. Sweeping the metal detector over the sandy bottom of the lake, she listened for any beeps.

Where is it? she thought, clenching her fist.

Without any light, the search was difficult.

I need help, she thought, feeling alone in the darkness.

Her locket popped open and warm objects brushed past her arms. Several purple orbs the size of golf balls sailed past her eyes.

Mom, you're back! Cordelia thought, regaining her confidence.

Her mother's voice emanated from the purple cluster. "I wish I could help you more, but at least I can provide some light."

Cordelia grinned. "Thanks, Mom."

"Be careful."

"I will."

Following the glowing purple lights, the metal detector started to beep. The beeps grew louder the farther she swam. Even though the water blurred her vision, she saw the shadowy outline of the ferry boat several feet ahead.

I found it!

A gaping hole went through the main deck and out the bottom of the ship as if it had been struck by a missile. Green algae covered the corroded guardrail. The top passenger area was exposed, but the bottom luggage area was buried in the sand.

The orbs swooped in a graceful arc and dropped inside the hole.

Cordelia followed closely behind. Weaving through the halls, the lights led her down to the bottom deck where the suitcases had been stowed.

A sudden current swept through the hallway, pushing her backward. Her body went into a backspin through an open doorway. The current slammed the door shut, pinning her tail between the door and doorframe. Cordelia clenched her eyes shut and whimpered in pain. The orbs spun around her body, appearing anxious over her predicament.

She tugged on her tail, hoping to pry herself loose. She wiggled her torso and flapped her tail, but the strong current held the wooden door closed.

I'm stuck!

She loosened the shovel from the shoulder strap and wedged the metal tip between the door and the frame. Using her upper body strength, she grunted and groaned as she pried the door open far enough to release her tail.

But the current slammed the door shut again.

"No!" she screamed underwater.

She pounded the tip of the shovel against the door. Little by little, she chipped away at the waterlogged door. The wood splinters floated away. With aching muscles, she carved out a hole larger than her body.

The orbs waited until Cordelia worked up the energy and the courage. She swam down the hall into the luggage room. She dropped the metal detector on the deck. Using the shovel, she dug into the sand. The hole kept caving in and each time she had to start over. She uncovered several suitcases, but none of them had Viktor's name on them.

I'm never going to find it! Cordelia thought; her frustration turned to fear.

Letting the current rock her body back and forth, she floated, closed her eyes, and rested her aching arms.

I should swim away! Forget the ribbon, forget the Olympics!

"Don't give up now," her mother's voice whispered. "You've come so far."

Cordelia's eyelids sprang open. The orbs danced before her eyes. A second wind kicked in and she dug deeper into the sand.

Clink, clink, clink!

Her shoulders tensed when the tip of the shovel struck a solid piece of metal. Using her hands, she scooped away the sand and uncovered a padlock and a suitcase. Water and sand had frayed the leather strips, but the suitcase was still intact. Underneath the handle was a metal pendant engraved with the name "Viktor Rusalka."

I found it! she thought. Her pulse raced.

She tugged and pulled on the handle, but the case was stuck. Swimming to the backside, she began digging. She jammed the tip of the shovel underneath the suitcase and pried it loose. The current grabbed the suitcase and it tumbled through the water. Cordelia gasped and swam after it, grabbing for the suitcase with each stroke.

Finally, her hand connected and gripped the suitcase handle.

I got the ribbon, now I'll get out of here!

Before she could swim away, the purple orbs collided together and formed into an image of her mom.

"Don't runaway," her mother said. "Your grandpa and Marcel are here. They're in grave danger and they need your help."

"Oh no!" Cordelia said. "Okay, Mom. I'll stay."

With a weary smile, her mother's image faded, leaving Cordelia alone in the cold darkness. Cordelia left the shovel and metal detector behind and swam out of the ship. The suitcase was heavy, but with her mermaid tail, she propelled herself toward the surface. Popping her head above the water, she swam toward the pier.

"Did you find it?" Rio yelled.

"Yes," Cordelia shouted back.

"Okay," Jack said. "Meet us on the beach."

Jack and Rio trekked east along the pier, climbed down the steps, and walked along the beach. Cordelia changed course and swam toward them. Jack waded in up to his knees and Cordelia handed him the water-logged suitcase. He grabbed it and returned to shore.

Keeping a close eye on the men, Cordelia rested in the shallows and propped her head above the water. Rio held up his flashlight

Traveling Circus and the Skeleton Key

while Jack tried opening the suitcase with the skeleton key. Sand and time had stiffened the lock. After a few shakes to get some of the water out of the keyhole, the key stiffly turned with a grinding noise. Jack opened the suitcase and pawed through the contents like a hungry dog looking for a bone. Old clothes scattered all over the beach.

Cordelia's heart sank when Jack shook the open suitcase upside down with no sign of the ribbon.

"It's not here," Jack groaned.

This can't be possible! Cordelia cursed under her breath.

"Check inside the pockets," Rio suggested.

Jack rummaged through the clothes reaching into all the pockets. He pulled out a thick roll of fabric.

"Is that it?" Rio asked.

Jack unrolled the ribbon onto the beach. Cordelia leaned forward, trying to take a closer look, but she was too far away to make out any of the letters.

"You found it!" Rio said.

Jack hunched over and began to read the spell out loud. Cordelia tried to make out the words, but his voice was too low to hear over the waves.

Several dark figures rustled along the tree line above them. Cordelia searched the darkness for the source of the noise.

"Grandpa?" she whispered.

Rio shined his flashlight along the ridge of the sand dunes. Cottonwood trees lined the ridge and dune grass covered the steep incline.

"Don't move and put your hands up!" a male's voice yelled from the hill.

Rio's flashlight lit up three officers running down the dune. One was a tall man with a rifle, another had a bushy mustache, and the other had a stocky frame. All three officers had their guns drawn.

As the police barreled forward, Jack thrust his hands into his laundry bag, pulled out four mice, and set them on the beach. After petting each one, the mice morphed and grew into three lions and lioness.

"Watch out!" Cordelia yelled to the officers, but her voice was barely audible above the churning waves.

Jack whistled and pointed toward the police. The animals bared their teeth and took off, kicking up the sand with their giant claws.

The tall policeman with a tranquilizer rifle came to a sudden halt at the bottom of the hill.

"Call them off or I'll shoot!" the tall man yelled and aimed his rifle.

Jack laughed, still holding onto the bag.

While the other two policemen aimed their guns, the tall officer fired his rifle. The tranquilizer dart caught the lioness in the shoulder. The wildcat wobbled for a minute and then collapsed to the ground with a loud thud.

A distant rumble came from the clouds to the east. Rio looked up at the sky, searching for the origin of the noise. The thudding sound grew louder.

Is that thunder? Cordelia wondered.

A helicopter swooped down from the clouds and a spotlight swept across the dunes. "Police" was written in bold white letters on the tail of the chopper. The metal blades kicked up sand and the wind stung Cordelia's eyes.

I'm saved! her heart filled with hope.

The side door on the helicopter slid open revealing an officer holding a tranquilizer rifle. A spark emitted from the barrel as the dart shot flew through the air and stuck itself in one of the lion's hind legs. Letting out a groan, the lion went limp and collapsed onto the sand.

As the helicopter circled over the water, Jack tossed the skeleton key to Rio. Shielding his face with his hand, Rio raised the skeleton key toward the sky. Thunder rolled through the clouds.

Cordelia's eyes widened. A bolt of lightning jumped from the tip of the key and struck the helicopter's tail rotor.

BOOM!

Cordelia covered her ears when the sound of crunching metal echoed through the cool night air. The helicopter shook, shimmied, and spun out of control. Flames erupted from the tail rotor and smoke billowed from the cockpit. The blades came to a screeching halt. The helicopter plummeted into the lake, creating giant waves that pushed Cordelia closer to the beach. A geyser of water sprayed 50 feet into the air and the droplets of water rained down on Cordelia's head. Her body bobbed up and down in the lake.

Wiping the water from her face, she spun around to see the three officers trapped by the two remaining lions. One lion held an officer pinned under its giant paws. With one hand on the barrel and the other on the stock, the officer held the rifle under the animal's chin.

A cop with the mustache backed away as the second lion inched closer and growled. The lion lunged forward and chomped down on his arm. He yelped in pain.

The third cop fired his gun and the bullet grazed the lion's shoulder blade. Startled, both lions backed away. The two officers helped the fallen one off the ground.

Jack whistled and pointed toward the officers. Both lions snapped to attention and chased the policemen down the pier toward the lighthouse.

Oh no! Cordelia thought when she saw the tranquilizer gun laying on the ground. *They dropped it!*

Running full-speed, one officer raised his walkie-talkie to his mouth and shouted, "We have an injured officer. We need backup and paramedics right now!"

Clutching his arm, the cop with the mustache tried his best to keep pace with his partners.

Running toward the dunes, Jack yelled, "We have the ribbon, let's get out of here!"

Rio followed close behind.

Cordelia desperately wanted to chase after them, but she couldn't leave the water. Feeling defeated, she watched the ribbon that could change her life travel up the dune in Jack's hand.

She heard faint cries for help. She looked back to where the helicopter had gone down and thought, *I need to save them before they drown.*

Like a torpedo, she sped toward the helicopter crash site.

22

The water churned and bubbled where the helicopter had plunged into the lake. Bobbing up and down, a man in a blue uniform waved his pale hand in the air. His face was red and he held onto a lifejacket to buoy himself in the water. A cracked helmet and debris floated with the waves.

"Are you hurt?" Cordelia called out, swimming closer to the man.

"I think my leg is broken," the man gasped.

"I'll take you to shore."

"Help the pilot first," the man said. "He's still down there."

She nodded and dove underwater. Large bubbles and cold water swirled around her body. Her vision was obscured by the pitch-black surroundings. Luckily, a purple orb brushed past her arm and guided her way. Fighting against the current, she zigzagged between twisted chunks of metal.

Broken in two, the helicopter lay on its side in a cloud of sand. The rotors were bent and the windshield had a crack shaped like a spider web. The pilot thrashed back and forth, caught in his seatbelt. One arm was bent and looked broken. With his face contorted in pain, he struggled to unbuckle the safety harness.

Cordelia sped to his rescue, unlatched the buckle, and pulled the pilot out of the cockpit. Grabbing the back of his belt, she propelled them toward the surface. Using the power of her tail, she pulled him parallel to the beach and pushed him closer to shallow water. He clawed his way to shore with his good arm. After he was safe, she turned around and swam back to the crash site to rescue the copilot.

∼

The cool wind brushed Flynn's cheeks and chilled his ears. Wishing he'd brought a warmer coat, his shoulders shivered. He raised his hands close to his mouth and blew hot air against his cold fingers. He hunched down behind the bushes with Rena and Albert at his side. He had high hopes when the police had arrived, but the three officers were chased away by the lions.

"I'm not waiting anymore!" Marcel said. "I'm going down there."

Marcel curled his weights until he stood nearly 12 feet tall.

"Wait for the others," Albert pleaded.

Before Albert finished his sentence, Marcel took off down the dune.

Gripping Flynn's shoulder, Rena gasped as they watch Jack and Rio running up the sand dunes straight toward them.

Jack and Rio stopped at the base of the dune when they saw Marcel barreling down the hill. Jack reached into his bag and pulled out two more mice. He quickly petted them and then dropped them onto the sand. The mice morphed and grew into two lions. They let out a ferocious roar, bared their sharp teeth, and ran straight for Marcel.

"Get the nets! Hurry!" Albert yelled. "I'll help Cordelia."

With flashlights in hand, Flynn and Rena jumped to their feet. Rena grabbed her backpack. Flynn loaded his flare gun, shoved it into his backpack, and chased after Marcel.

Halfway down the hill, one lion leapt into the air and clawed at Marcel's chest. Marcel cried out in pain as he spun around, fell to his knees, and wrestled the animal to the ground. The other lion jumped on his back. With a wide-open jaw, the beast clamped down on Marcel's neck. Marcel swatted with his massive hands, but the animals tightened their grips and didn't let go.

Standing a safe distance away, Flynn and Rena watched as Marcel wrestled with the lions.

"Get the nets ready!" Flynn said.

Marcel rolled over on his side, pinning the one lion underneath his shoulders. It growled and thrashed its legs. Marcel ripped the other lion off his chest, threw it aside, and kicked the animal with his foot. The lion shook its head and let out a whimper.

"Quick!" Rena said. "Throw the net."

Flynn clumsily opened the net with one hand and threw the bundle of rope in the air, but the net fell short.

Rena ran with the open net and threw it. Flynn cheered when the net dropped over the lion. The lion tried running, but its legs were tangled. The animal twisted, turned, and struggled to break free.

Rena and Flynn jumped back when it let out a loud growl. The lion hissed and clawed at Rena's hand as she cautiously tied the loose ends of the net with some rope.

"I hope that'll hold em," Rena said, wiping her brow.

"Me too," Flynn replied.

The second lion still clung to Marcel's back. Using his upper body strength, Marcel slammed the lion against the hill until it let go. A geyser of sand shot into the air. Marcel rose to his feet, grabbed the stunned animal, and launched it into the air. With a howl, the animal flew several hundred feet and landed with a giant splash in Lake Michigan.

Holding a hand over the bite marks on his neck, Marcel lumbered forward. His movements were sluggish and his chest heaved with each passing breath.

∽

Cordelia pushed the helicopter copilot into shallower water.

"Thanks for saving us," the pilot said as he helped his friend to shore.

Cordelia pushed back her wet hair from her eyes and said, "You're welcome."

She heard Albert call out her name. She turned her head and saw Albert running down the beach, nearly losing his balance on the uneven sand. With sore shoulders, she swam closer to him.

Albert waded into the water and asked, "Are you okay?"

"Grandpa! Yes, I am," Cordelia said with a hoarse voice.

Looking over Albert's shoulder, she saw Rio lift the skeleton key and point it at Marcel.

"Look out!" Cordelia yelled, but she was too far away.

Rena and Flynn jumped out of the way and tumbled down the hill, kicking up sand with their sneakers.

Marcel rolled to the ground as a lightning bolt struck directly behind his head. Sparks exploded like a firework show. The dry dune grass burst into flames and the fire began to spread.

With tight lips and narrowed eyes, Marcel's muscles rippled. He stood and barreled forward ready to fight.

The tip of the key glowed orange and another shot of lightning struck the ground beneath Marcel's feet. The shockwave knocked Marcel to his knees. He tripped and fell face first into the sand. His body rolled all the way down the steep dune. His head smacked against a driftwood log on the beach. With his arms and legs sprawled out, he slowly shrunk down to regular size. He didn't move a muscle or raise his head.

"No!" Cordelia screamed.

Tears welled in her eyes as she pounded her fist against the water's surface.

She dove back underwater and swam closer to Marcel as Albert sprinted along the beach. Cordelia wished she could run to Marcel's side. Instead, she was stuck in the water, swishing her tail back in forth.

I wish I could run to his side, she thought.

～

Flynn and Rena stood silhouetted in the moonlight. Orange lights twinkled to life on the side of the dune. The embers started to glow and burst into flames. Dried driftwood and brown beach grass caught on fire and inched closer to Flynn and Rena. Flynn heard a growl and the bushes rustled. After chasing away the three police officers, the two lions from earlier had returned!

"Run!" Rena yelled.

With his knees shaking, Flynn ran as fast as he could down the hill. His flashlight battery was low and the bulb dimmed. Running blindly in the dark, Flynn tripped and fell into a thick clump of tall grass. Flynn groaned when he bumped his injured wrist. Rena ran up beside him, offered her hand, and helped him stand-up just before the dune grass caught fire. The flames scorched his pant leg and the acrid smoke filled his lungs.

Flynn and Rena ran along the beach to Marcel. Looking over his shoulder, Flynn saw Jack waving his hand and whistling for his trained lions.

Flynn looked down at Marcel. His body and muscles lay motionless on the beach.

"What do we do?" Flynn asked.

"Draw a first aid kit," Rena said

Flynn had no idea how to treat the bite and claw marks.

"He needs a doctor not a drawing," Flynn replied.

"He's bleeding," Rena said, pointing to Marcel's neck.

Spots of blood dotted his chest.

"Are you okay?" Flynn said, tapping Marcel's shoulder. "Wake up. We gotta go."

Marcel didn't move a muscle. Rena checked his pulse.

No, don't leave us, Flynn thought. Despite Marcel's past mistakes, he had always been there to help Cordelia.

"I feel a faint pulse," Rena said, coughing up smoke.

Flynn let out a sigh of relief.

"We can't stay here," Rena said with desperation in her eyes.

"We can't leave him here alone on the beach."

Rena ripped part of her shirt into strips and wrapped Marcel's wounds.

The fire crackled and smoke filled the air. Between the water and the trees, the dune grass was engulfed in flames. Jack, Rio, and the lions turned north and ran toward the pier, but the dry bushes and wood boardwalk caught fire and created a wall of flames. The men and animals stopped, turned around, and sprinting south along the beach.

Flynn glanced over his shoulder to see Albert running and waving his arms.

Cordelia's head popped up from a wave and yelled, "Is Marcel okay?"

"He's hurt badly," Rena shouted. "But I felt a pulse."

Fire leapt up from the dune grass and spread to a nearby tree. Flames licked at the cottonwood trees and rippled through the dry grass like a deadly wind. Sparks and smoke flew into the sky. The heat raised the air temperature a few degrees.

Jack, Rio, and the lions were illuminated by the fire, stuck in a wide pocket of sand, and surrounded by smoldering dune grass. The blaze flowed along the ridge and cut off the space between the shore and the dunes. The only way out was to run past Rena and Flynn.

"They're coming right for us," Rena's voice crackled. "What do we do now?"

Albert ran up to them, bent over, and placed his hands on his knees.

Catching his breath, Albert asked, "Flynn can you stop them?"

"What can I draw?" Flynn asked, shrugging his shoulders.

23

The pungent smell of burning wood rose into the air, making everyone cough.

"Maybe Flynn and I can clear a path for everyone," Cordelia said.

"How?" Rena asked.

"Flynn, you draw some fire extinguishers and I'll splash water on the flames near the shore," Cordelia suggested.

"Here." Flynn pulled out the flare gun from his backpack and handed it to Cordelia. "Take this out into the water and fire it. Maybe the police, Paula, and Rego will see it."

She nodded. Carrying the gun above the water, she swam 100 yards away from the shore, stopped, and fired it into the sky.

POW!

The flare burst into the air and exploded into a fireball. Red sparks arced back down, hit the water, and vanished.

Using the light from the flames, Flynn sat down on the beach and began to draw. His fingers and arm were swollen as he tried holding the pencil steady.

He gritted his teeth, held his throbbing wrist, and thought, *I wish I had my pain meds.*

His adrenaline overpowered his pain and he drew a cylindrical metal tube and nozzle. Within a few moments, the drawing turned into a real fire extinguisher. He rested his sore wrist while Rena grabbed the container and fought the wall of fire.

Cordelia disappeared into the waves. Soon, giant splashes erupted from the lake and water sprayed over the sand. She traveled up and down along the beach, splashing on the flames. Despite all their efforts, the fire still raged on.

Feeling defeated, Flynn's shoulders slumped and his hope faded. Rena jumped back as a smoldering tree landed with a thud next to her. She dropped the extinguisher and scurried to Flynn's side. The heat warmed Flynn's cheeks and radiated through his clothing.

A wailing siren echoed through the crisp night air, growing louder with each passing second. Red and blue lights bounced around the trees at the top of the hill. Flynn's spirit soared when he saw several firemen lined up in formation, carrying fire hoses. He raised a fist into the air and cheered.

The sound of pressure pumps drawing water from the channel echoed through the night air. The valves on the fire hose gushed open and cooling mist landed on Flynn's hot cheek. The fire fizzled and snapped as gallons of water rained down on the flames. The glowing embers faded and billowing smoke rose into the air.

With a wide grin, Flynn looked at Rena and said, "Reinforcements!"

She tapped his shoulder and pointed, "But they're still coming for us!"

Flynn turned and saw Jack thrust his hand into his laundry bag and fish around inside. Jack came up empty-handed and then he threw away the bag. With a scowl, he turned to his trained lions and petted each one.

"What is he doing?" Flynn asked.

Rena jumped back in shock as the lion's claws turned into hooves, the legs grew long and thin, and the fur changed colors. The lions morphed into two full-size horses.

"Come on!" Jack yelled. He leapt up on the horse's back. "Let's get out of here."

The horse tossed its head and shied away from the fire, but Jack took a firm hold on its mane and urged it forward with a kick. Jack's eyes narrowed and his face was twisted in a sneer as the horse galloped south along the beach.

Traveling Circus and the Skeleton Key

Rio mounted the other horse and nudged the animal with his heel. The horses snapped to attention and barreled straight for Rena, Flynn, and Albert.

Raising his hand in the air, Rio pointed the key toward the ground near Flynn's feet. A lightning bolt jumped from the tip of the key and struck the ground with a blinding flash.

Albert and Rena jumped out of the way, landing on a mound of sand. Frightened, Flynn ran into the water, tripped, and fell face first into a big wave. Flynn propped himself on his hands and knees. His clothes were drenched in water.

With a clear path, Jack's horse leapt over Marcel's limp body and galloped forward. Rio followed close behind. The hooves pounded the sand like a steady drum beat as the horses disappeared into the darkness.

"They're getting away!" Albert groaned.

"Need some help?" asked a familiar voice from above.

Everyone looked up in the air. Flapping their large wings and carrying Sammy and Buster in their arms, Paula and Rego dropped down from the sky like two large birds. Their white feathers rippled in the wind as they swooped down and set the two clowns on the beach.

"You made it," Albert said with a wide grin.

"Better late than never," Paula said, fluttering over everyone's head.

"The police are on their way," Rego said. "How can we help?"

"Jack escaped with the scroll," said Albert, pointing south.

Reaching into her back pack, Rena pulled out the last net.

"Here," Rena said, raising it into the air. "Use this."

Rego swooped down and grabbed the net.

"Let's get 'em," Paula said to Rego.

He nodded as they flew after the horses. Sammy and Buster ran along the shore. Cordelia swam after the horses, keeping a close eye on Jack.

Rio looked over his shoulder and noticed Paula and Rego hot on their heels. He raised the skeleton key over his head.

"Watch out!" Cordelia yelled.

Traveling Circus and the Skeleton Key

Several lightning bolts shot from the key, zigzagging in all directions. Paula and Rego shot through the air, dodging the bolts and sparks.

Rego swooped down, circled around the horse, and kicked Rio in the shoulder. The horse came to a sudden halt and rose on its hind legs. Rio lost his grip, slid off the horse, and tumbled to the ground. The skeleton key flew from Rio's hands and landed on the sand.

Paula swooped down and snatched the key off the beach.

"No!" Rio shouted.

Rego flapped his wings high overhead, held the net with both hands, and lined up the shot. Rio tried to run into the darkness, but Rego swooped down like an eagle after his prey and dropped the net over him. Rio tripped, fell, and tangled in the mesh. The horse ran off and vanished into the woods.

"Perfect shot!" Paula yelled, giving him a thumbs-up.

Paula and Rego landed and tied the loose ends of the net. Rio tried kicking himself free, but the ends were drawn tight.

Sammy and Buster, who had been chasing them, finally caught up.

"Jack's getting away," Cordelia shouted and pointed toward Jack's horse galloping down the shore.

"Lasso," Buster said, holding out his hand.

Sammy lay down on the sand, stretched, and twisted his body into a long thin rope. Buster picked Sammy off the ground and spun him over his head like a cowboy's lasso. Buster released Sammy into the air. The rope arced into the air and landed around the neck of Jack's horse. Buster dug his heels into the sand and pulled the horse to a halt.

Before Jack could dismount, Buster let go of the rope. Sammy's body snapped like a sling-shot, sailed through the air, and wrapped around Jack. Sammy's rubbery arms and legs trapped Jack like he was caught in a spider web.

Sammy stuck his head over Jack's shoulder and yelled, "Got him!"

"Yay!" Cordelia shouted.

Paula grabbed Jack by the feet and flew back to Albert. Rego

Traveling Circus and the Skeleton Key

swooped down, grabbed the ends of the net, and dragged Rio down the beach. Jack and Rio kicked and cursed all the way.

Cordelia swam parallel to the shore.

When she was within earshot, she turned to Albert and said, "Grandpa, I found a ribbon on the sunken ship. The ribbon has a spell that will help us control our powers."

Albert's eyes widened and he raised his fist in the air. "That's the answer we've been looking for! First we'll take away Jack's powers and then I'll help you!"

"Me too!" Flynn beamed.

Cordelia grinned from ear to ear. *I'll get my life back!*

"Who has the scroll?" Rego demanded with a scowl.

"Jack has it," Cordelia said.

Rego rummaged through Jack's pockets and found the scroll and ribbon.

"You're going to regret this," Jack grunted, shaking his head.

"No," Rego replied. "You're going back to jail. This time for good!"

With all the items in hand, Rego offered the clowns a quick salute and handed the ribbon and scroll back to Albert for safe keeping. Paula brought the key to Albert.

"Well done," Albert said, patting her shoulder.

Albert stood over Jack and unrolled the Secret Talent Scroll

"I need some light," Albert said.

Flynn shined his flashlight over Albert's shoulder.

"I call upon the four classical elements: Wind, fire, earth, and water," he read the spell. "Wind moves sand. Fire creates earth and ash. Earth absorbs water. Water quenches fire. Remove Jack's power to change any animal into another animal."

With narrowed eyes, Jack squirmed in Sammy's rope-like arms and yelled, "No!"

Albert turned to Rio and repeated the spell. The tip of the skeleton key no longer glowed orange and the metal turned cold.

"Who would like to do the honors?" Albert asked, holding up the key.

Flynn took the key from Albert's hand and threw it far into

Lake Michigan.

Looking defeated, Rio shook his fist and kicked his feet in protest. He was powerless under the weight of the net.

Wasting no time taking off his shoes, Albert waded into the water and stood next to Cordelia. Flynn held the flashlight while Albert unrolled the ribbon and read the spell.

"The scroll unlocked the power within you. Use this power to help people, instead of only yourself. I call upon the four elements—wind, fire, earth, and water—to remove Cordelia's limiting beliefs and control the power within."

A flutter of electricity pulsed through her body and then a warm felling washed her body. Cordelia swam closer to the beach in shallower water. She imagined her tail turning into legs. Her scales slid back underneath her skin as her tail morphed into feet and split into two legs. Cold water lapped against her bare legs under the pale moonlight.

With a sudden rush of joy, Cordelia jumped out of the water, stretched her leg muscles, and stood on her own two legs.

"I'm free! The curse is broken!" she shouted with a wide grin.

Cordelia heard Marcel groan. Worried, she rushed over to his motionless body on the beach.

24

Cordelia knelt down next to Marcel and placed her hand on his back. She felt his spine move up and down with each passing breath. He lay motionless on the beach sand.

"Where are the paramedics?" Cordelia asked with a furrowed brow.

"When we flew over, we saw a few ambulances heading this way," Rego said reassuringly.

Cordelia rubbed Marcel's shoulder and bit her lip. Albert knelt down beside her and placed his hand on her shoulder.

"He's going to be okay," Albert said. "We'll get him to the hospital and the doctors will patch him up."

"Okay," Cordelia said. "But what about the evidence that could help clear Dad's name?"

"Where's the evidence?" Albert glared at Jack.

"You'll never find it," Jack sneered. "I told my wife to burn the evidence."

"Grandpa, someone needs to track her down and stop her," Cordelia pleaded.

"Tell us where she went," Albert grunted.

"Never," Jack sputtered.

"Jack, are you afraid of heights?" Rego asked with a mischievous grin.

Jack's eyes widened.

Rego looked at Sammy and said, "Let go of him."

Traveling Circus and the Skeleton Key

Sammy unwrapped his thin rope-like body from around Jack and let him go.

Before Jack could run away, Rego snatched him by the back of his belt and leapt into the sky. They flew high into the clouds. Rego zigzagged through the clouds as Jack's arms and legs flailed.

Way up in the clouds, Rego let go. With his arms and legs flailing, Jack shrieked as he plummeted to the earth. In the nick of time, Rego swooped down and caught Jack just before he hit the beach. Rego flew in a lazy circle and then landed.

Sammy wrapped his rubbery arms around Jack's arms and held him captive.

"He cooperated after I dropped him." Rego laughed.

"What did he say?" Paula asked.

"He gave me his home address," Rego said. "His wife, Shirley, is there waiting for him. He said the ledgers are in the barn."

"Shirley was the getaway driver," Cordelia said. "Jack sent her home along with Murphy to load up their belongings and burn the evidence. Their plan was to escape to Russia."

Albert looked at Cordelia and said, "Okay, go with Marcel to the hospital. I'll stay here and talk to the police. They can get a search warrant for the evidence and stop Shirley from escaping."

Cordelia nodded.

Albert turned to Flynn and said, "First I need to help you. I'll use the ribbon spell on you, so you can go home."

Flynn felt a wave relief. He looked at Rena and smiled.

Albert held the ribbon in his hands, and repeated the spell:

"The scroll unlocked the power within you. Use this power to help people, instead of only yourself. I call upon the four elements, wind, fire, earth, and water, to remove Flynn and Rena's limiting beliefs and control the power within."

Flynn felt a tingling sensation run through his body. For a few moments, the pain in his wrist subsided.

"Now, you can draw your own world," Albert said, patting Flynn on the shoulder.

Flynn felt chills just thinking about the endless possibilities.

"When you first gave me my power, how did you know I wasn't

going to do something bad?" Flynn asked.

"Giving you a power was a risk," Albert said. "But I hoped you would use it to find your courage. You've done good things with your talents. You should be proud of yourself."

"Thank you," Flynn replied. "Wish we had more time to say goodbye."

Feeling sad, Flynn reached out to shake Albert's hand. Instead, Albert leaned in and gave Flynn a hug.

"I owe you a lot," Albert said with tears in his eyes. "You saved the circus."

"I wanted to help," Flynn replied.

Albert let go of their embrace and smiled.

"Oh wait," Flynn said. "I almost forgot."

Flynn reached into his pocket and pulled out Salvatore's watch. Albert held up his hands and stumbled backward.

"You found it," Albert said. "The police never released my son's belongings. How did you fix it?"

"The pocket watch ended up at an antique repair shop and they fixed it. I bought it so I could destroy it."

Albert put his hands on his hips and scowled.

"Do you want it?" Flynn asked.

With trembling hands, Albert reached out and took the watch.

"Okay," Albert said. "I'll take care of it."

Rena looked at her own watch and said, "We're late."

Flynn nodded.

"I guess this is goodbye," Flynn said.

"Until we meet again," Albert said with a weary smile.

Albert turned to Rego and asked, "Can you take them back to their car?"

"Sure," Rego said.

Paula and Rego stretched out their wings and wrapped their arms around Flynn and Rena. Flynn's feet lifted off the ground and dangled in the breeze. With the wind whistling in his ears, Flynn watched the beach and pier shrink from his view.

The dune grass and driftwood smoldered and musty smoke lingered in the air. Cordelia watched the firemen slowly bring the flames under control.

Sammy unwrapped his rope-like body from around Jack. Buster reached out and grabbed Jack's elbows.

"You're not going anywhere," Buster growled and tightened his grip. "Don't get any ideas."

Sammy's body expanded like a balloon and returned to his normal form.

The two officers from earlier returned. With flashlights in their hands, they jogged down the sand dune and sprinted over to Jack and Rio,

The stocky officer looked at the clowns and asked, "Who are you?"

"I'm Sammy and this is my brother Buster," Sammy said.

Sammy pointed to Jack and Rio and said, "They escaped from prison this morning and held my friend, Cordelia, hostage."

"Yes," the stocky officer said. "We issued an APB this morning. We've been looking for these guys. Albert called us this afternoon and gave us a tip on where to find them. Jack and Rio are considered armed and dangerous."

The tall officer read Jack and Rio their Miranda rights and handcuffed the two men.

Four paramedics ran down the hill, carrying stretchers and medical bags. Two attended to the officers from the helicopter and the others came over to Marcel.

Dressed in a dark blue uniform, a tall woman with blonde hair pulled into a ponytail kneeled beside Marcel and took his pulse. A rugged paramedic with spiked brown hair taped bandages over Marcel's wounds. They gently rolled him onto the stretcher and placed an oxygen mask over his mouth.

"Is he going to be okay?" Cordelia's voice cracked.

"He has a nasty bump on his head" the rugged paramedic said. "It might be a concussion."

"Can I go with him to the hospital?" Cordelia asked.

"Are you his girlfriend?" the blonde woman asked.

Cordelia hesitated for a moment, bowed her head, and nodded. It was first time she ever admitted it to herself.

The paramedics gently lifted the stretcher and carried Marcel to the concrete pier. They lowered the stretcher legs to the pavement and rolled Marcel toward the lighthouse parking lot. Cordelia walked alongside, holding Marcel's hand. Looking over her shoulder, Cordelia saw Jack giving her a menacing stare.

Albert ran up beside Cordelia.

In a hushed tone, Albert asked, "Are you going to be okay?"

Cordelia nodded.

"Good," Albert said. "When I'm done here, I'll meet you at the hospital."

Cordelia nodded. She stayed with Marcel and hoped for the best.

25

Flynn looked at his throbbing wrist. The compression brace was dirty from the smoke and charred grass. The adrenaline and excitement had worn off, leaving Flynn sore and tired. He stared out the car window as Rena drove into his parents' driveway. Neither of them had said much on the ride home.

Rena parked the car and turned off the engine. "What a crazy night, huh?"

"Yeah, never a dull moment."

He reached into the back seat and grabbed his burnt backpack. He hoped his parents didn't notice the smoky smell and start asking questions.

"Life is always an adventure with you," Rena said.

Flynn chuckled.

Rena fidgeted in her seat, gripped the steering wheel, and made quick glances at Flynn. He smiled back at her, unbuckled the seatbelt, and slid closer to her.

"Rena?" Flynn said.

She looked deep into his eyes. "Yes?"

He leaned in and kissed her.

"Thanks for going with me tonight," he said.

"Anytime. But next time we hangout, we're going to the movies."

"Deal," Flynn said. "I better go. My parents are waiting for me."

If his parents weren't spying on him, Flynn would've kissed her again.

I can't wait for our next date, he thought with a wide smile.

The porch light flipped on and the front door burst open. Flynn's parents stormed out outside. Ray scowled and Georgia pointed to the watch on her wrist. They came to a halt in front of Rena's car.

"Get out of the car, Flynn!" Ray growled, tapping his finger on the car hood.

Bright headlights flashed in the rearview mirror. Flynn turned around. A work truck pulled into the driveway and parked behind Rena's car. Gainsborough Homebuilders was written in bold white letters on the truck door.

"Oh no," Rena gasped. "We're in trouble."

Flynn and Rena slid out of the car. With slumped shoulders, Flynn leaned against the fender and stared at the ground.

Flynn's knees trembled. "Sorry we're late."

"Where have you been?" Ray demanded with a stern stare.

"We were worried sick," Georgia said, crossing her arms.

Mr. and Mrs. Gainsborough jumped out of the truck and ran up to Rena. Dressed in a button-up blouse, Mrs. Gainsborough placed her manicured hands on her hips and shook her head. She looked like she was going to a dinner party, not a late-night argument.

"You both have some explaining to do," Mr. Gainsborough said. His bald head turned red and his jowl quivered.

"Well," Flynn said, taking a big gulp of air. "The circus came back into town."

"Oh no," Mrs. Gainsborough groaned. "Again?"

"What kind of trouble are you in now?" Ray sighed and leaned forward.

"Instead of going to the movies, we were with the circus," Flynn said with his voice cracking.

"What?" Ray stammered. "This is unacceptable."

"But we have good news," Rena said. "Albert found a way to help us control our powers."

"Yes," Flynn added. "Albert helped us."

"I can control my music!" Rena added.

Georgia's face lit up and she said, "That's great news."

"Yes, it's good news, Flynn, but you can't just run off without telling us," Ray said. "Your mom and I might have to ground you for this."

"I understand," Flynn said, looking up at his dad.

"I'm happy that you can control your powers," Mr. Gainsborough said, rubbing Rena's shoulder. "But we'll talk about your punishment when we get home, okay?"

"Yes, Dad," Rena mumbled.

"It will be awhile before you two can hangout alone," Ray added.

"Can we still talk on the phone?" Flynn asked.

"If it's okay with Rena's parents, you can call each other," Georgia said.

Mrs. Gainsborough looked at her husband. He shrugged his shoulders.

"Yes, it's okay," Mrs. Gainsborough said. "But it'll be awhile before you can be alone together."

Flynn let out a sigh of relief. Rena gave him a half smile. It wasn't the outcome Flynn wanted, but at least they could still see each other.

"Come on, Rena," Mr. Gainsborough said. "It's time to go home; it's late."

Flynn walked over to the driver's side door and gave Rena a quick hug. Rena gave him a wink and smile, hopped into her car, and followed her parents home.

Ray placed his hand on Flynn's shoulder, "You need to call us if you're going to be late."

"Okay, Dad. I will next time."

26

The hospital bustled with nurses and doctors moving in and out of examining rooms. Cordelia rocked back and forth in her seat. With his eyes closed, Marcel lay on the bed with a bandage wrapped around his head and an oxygen mask strapped around his nose and mouth to counter the effects of the smoke inhalation.

Feeling tired, Cordelia found a small space on the bed. She lowered the guard rail and crawled up next to Marcel. Without disturbing the air hose, she slid her arm across his chest. Laying her head on the pillow, she wiggled her toes and stretched her legs. It felt good to lie in a real bed.

I hope Marcel is going to be okay, Cordelia thought as she drifted into a deep sleep.

Cordelia's eyes fluttered open and she found Marcel's big brown eyes staring back at her. He stroked her hair with his free hand.

"You're okay!" Her throat tightened. A wave of relief swept over her. "I was worried about you."

She hugged him.

"Ow," Marcel winced.

"Sorry!" She started to let go, but he held her.

"It's okay," he said.

"Thank you for saving me," she sniffed, wiping away a tear.

"We did it together," he whispered.

Marcel leaned in and kissed her.

Cordelia looked up into his eyes. "And now we're free."

"What do you mean?" he asked.

"I found a ribbon on the sunken boat," she said. "The ribbon has another spell that gives you the ability to control the power within yourself."

"Really?" Marcel raised his eyebrows. "Will it work for me?"

"Yes," she said with a wide grin. "It worked on me."

"Awesome!" he said, hugging her with his good arm. "I can start training again. Now we have a shot at the Olympics!"

Cordelia heard a gentle knock on the door. She looked up and saw Albert enter the room. He sat down in a chair next to the bed and leaned back. He rested his elbows on his knees and rubbed his face with his hands.

Cordelia slid out of the hospital bed and kneeled down beside her grandpa's chair.

"Is everything okay?" Cordelia asked.

"It's over," Albert whispered. "The police obtained a search warrant. They found the evidence to free your dad. They also found books on how to train exotic animals."

"That's how Jack knows so much about animals," Marcel said.

A single tear escaped Cordelia's eye and cascaded down her cheek.

I have my family and my life back. Cordelia's heart filled with hope.

Albert reached into his pocket, pulled out the ribbon, and unrolled it on his lap.

"Now it's time to help Marcel," Albert whispered.

Marcel's eyes widened as Albert read the spell on the ribbon.

27

September 18
Naples, Florida

Paintings of athletes hung on the walls and on the desk was a nameplate that read Coach Neiman. The cool air from the air conditioner in the office made Cordelia shiver. Marcel's chair squeaked as he tapped his foot on the tile floor. Albert, sitting between the two of them and directly in front of the coach's desk, gripped the armrests.

"I know you're the swim coach," Albert said. "But thank you for helping us find a trainer for Marcel."

"No problem," Coach Neiman said. "Glad I could help."

"Any word on how Marcel can compete in the qualifiers?" Albert asked.

"I spoke with the Olympic officials," Coach Neiman said. "They agreed to retest Marcel for chemicals in his system. If the results come back negative, he can compete in the qualification process."

"That's great news," Albert said, rubbing Marcel's shoulder.

"When can I take the test?" Marcel asked.

"Anytime," Coach Neiman replied. "Just as long as the lab results arrive at the Olympic headquarters before trials, you'll be in good shape."

Marcel let out a sigh of relief.

"Here's a list of tests your doctor will need to perform," Coach Neiman said, handing Marcel a packet of papers. "And here's the address to send the results."

"Great," Albert said. "Thank you. I'll take Marcel to his doctor right away."

"Good. The sooner the better," Coach Neiman said. "The next scouting camp for potential Olympic athletes is this October in Michigan."

Cordelia nodded. "It's at the Delta Training and Swim Center in Grand Rapids, right?"

The coach nodded.

Albert smiled. "Guess we'll be making a trip back to Michigan."

"Hopefully," said Marcel, staring at the paperwork in his hand.

~

September 25
Naples, Florida

Cordelia waited outside Coach Neiman's office for Marcel. The test results weighed on her mind. Through the thin office door, she heard bits and pieces of what they were saying. She was trying not to pry, but she was anxious to hear the results.

If he can't compete, I'll feel awful, she thought. *I want him to be there! He might not even want to go out anymore if I'm competing and he can't.*

She slumped against the wall. Within minutes her fingers were tapping and she couldn't stand still. She fiddled with the zipper on her backpack in an attempt to calm her nerves.

The voices inside became low, too quiet to hear. Cordelia stood still, straining to hear any hint of what was going on inside. She heard footsteps beyond the wall. Cordelia managed to dodge aside just in time to avoid being hit by the door flying open.

Marcel stood there with a big grin on his face. The doctor had removed the stitches from his back and chest, and his wounds were beginning to scar over.

"Can you compete?" Cordelia asked.

"Yes." He picked her up and spun her around. "I can't wait to tell my parents the news. They'll be happy."

Cordelia smiled as he took her hand and they all but ran to the parking lot.

~

October 12
Delta Training and Swim Center in Grand Rapids, Michigan

Albert stood with Cordelia and Marcel in the bustling lobby of the Delta Center. Hundreds of athletes carrying duffle bags and wearing warm-up suits poured into the building. She looked around at all the doors and hallways, reading the signs.

"I'm guessing the two of you will need to change, warm up, and find your places," Albert said. "I'm going to find a good seat. Good luck to the both of you."

Albert hugged Cordelia and shook Marcel's hand. Albert walked over to the front desk, picked up the event schedule, and disappeared into the crowd.

Marcel shouldered his gym bag and gave Cordelia a quick kiss on the cheek. "Nervous?"

"A little. But we can control our powers and we have a chance to qualify."

Marcel straightened his shoulders and said, "You'll do great."

"You too," she said with butterflies swirling in her stomach.

Marcel headed for the men's locker rooms. Cordelia watched him go for a moment before going to the women's area.

~

Cordelia reviewed the event schedule that was posted on the wall inside the women's locker room. Her spirits sank when she saw Marcel's timeslot overlapped hers.

I'm going to miss his competition, she frowned.

She thought about all the years of her parents driving her to pool practice, her mother spending the school year apart from her

Traveling Circus and the Skeleton Key

father, and the time spent in Florida.

It all comes down to this day, she thought.

The pressure weighed on her shoulders. Her eyes began to cloud as she took off her shoes and put them in a locker. On autopilot, she unzipped her bag, and changed into her swimsuit. Feeling dizzy, her face grew hot and her hands trembled. Cordelia fumbled her way to the row of sinks and splashed water on her face.

"Are you okay?" asked the girl at the sink beside her.

"Just nerves," Cordelia said without thinking.

"I'm sure you'll be great," the girl said with a smile.

The loud nervous chatter around her faded into the background as the other swimmers exited out the door. The locker room became eerily quiet. Cordelia splashed more water on her face. Looking up at the mirror, she watched water droplets fall from her chin and her reflection rippled like waves on a pond.

Am I hallucinating? Cordelia thought, rubbing her eyes.

She flinched when her locket popped open. Purple orbs floated out of the locket, splashed against the mirror, and created a purple ghostly image of her mother.

"Mom, I'm afraid," Cordelia whispered.

Gala's soothing voice said, "Don't worry, honey, you can do this."

"What if I fail again?"

"Learn from your mistakes," Gala whispered. "You won't fail. You've worked so hard. Now, close your eyes and concentrate."

Closing her eyes, Cordelia nodded.

"Now imagine yourself performing well in the competition," her mom said. "Be specific and detailed in your thoughts."

The movement of her arms, legs, and body replayed in Cordelia's mind. She remembered the way the water felt on her skin and the smell of the chlorine. How the repetition of her stroke and the flutter kick of her legs pushed her faster through the pool. And at the end, she imagined the sweet victory of surpassing her record time.

Cordelia splashed cold water on her face again and rubbed her eyes. The image of her mom faded. The orbs floated back inside her locket and the cover closed. Cordelia's stomach settled and her eyes became clear. Standing straight and tall, she headed for the pool.

~

Breathing in a rhythm and shaking out her fingers, Cordelia stared at the ripples on the pool's surface. No visions of her mom appeared. Instead, Cordelia replayed all her swim techniques from her coach.

Just like practice. I can do this. Cordelia breathed silently.

Beep!

Cordelia dove off the diving block into the pool. Letting her muscles take over, she cut through the water like a shark. The seconds flew by. She reached the opposite end, flipped underwater, and shot back to the starting point.

Popping her head above the water, she looked at time clock.

52.2 seconds! Cordelia felt ecstatic. *I have a good chance to make the team!*

She dried off with a towel, raced up the bleachers, and gave her grandpa a hug.

"Congratulations," Albert beamed with pride.

"Thanks," she said. "Is Marcel done with his competition?"

"I don't know," Albert said.

"Okay, let's go find out."

Albert nodded and followed her out of the pool area into the hall.

"Which gym is he competing in?" she asked. "I was getting ready and I didn't have time to look at a map."

Albert nodded. "Follow me."

They wove through the crowded hall and passed between gyms. Cordelia spotted the auditorium where Marcel's event was scheduled. She darted down the hall and plowed straight into someone's chest. Looking up, her eyes met Marcel's smile.

"Did you compete yet? I wanted to watch," she blurted.

He grinned. "I did. I made the team!"

Albert caught up to them both. "That's wonderful news.

Congratulations!"

"Thank you, sir," Marcel beamed with pride. "I owe you a lot."

"You're welcome," Albert said.

28

October 16
Whitehall, Michigan

Flynn reread the paperwork from Professor Copley:

The deadline for submission is October 17. All artwork must be delivered to Grand River Art and Music College no later than 12 pm.

This is it! Flynn worried. *One last night to finish it.*

For the past month he had struggled to complete a new painting as he watched the days tick by. After the doctor had removed the wrist brace, Flynn could paint in short sessions before his hand started to ache. Oil paints take time to dry, giving Flynn time to rest his wrist.

His trembling fingers held the paintbrush. Without the brace, his hand felt awkward. His brush strokes became sporadic, gone were the fluid lines.

The open book with the photo of his inspirational painting sat on the desk.

Will anyone see the similarity to the Winslow Homer painting "The Gulf Stream"? Flynn wondered.

The water and the stormy sky created an ominous tone. Tonight he would add the finishing touches on the boat and the highlights on the waves.

His mother stopped by his open bedroom door. "How's it coming along? Is it ready?"

"I'm still working on it," he groaned.

"It's due tomorrow," Georgia said with stress in her voice. She stepped inside his room. "Maybe you should submit it next year?"

"No," Flynn sternly replied. "I've come so far."

She placed her hand on his shoulder and squeezed.

"I love the details in the water. I can't wait to see it finished, but don't strain yourself."

She held up a clear plastic bag with ice and said, "I brought you some ice just in case you needed it."

"Thanks, Mom."

With a concerned look, she placed a towel on his desk and set the bag of ice on top. She backed out of the room and quietly closed the door behind her.

Flynn turned on the lamp next to his bed. His muscles tightened and his fingers felt numb. Blocking out the discomfort, he dipped his brush back into the light teal and continued to paint. The hours ticked by and the crickets chirped.

Somewhere in the early morning hours, he collapsed onto the bed and fell into a deep sleep. His mind drifted into nightmares about failing the competition.

～

The sunlight sifted through the window pane and warmed Flynn's cheek. He lifted one eyelid and looked at the time: 11am.

Oh no! he thought as he jumped out of bed. *I must've overslept!*

Splattered paint was in his hair, on his hands, and clothes. His eyes slowly adjusted to the morning light and he realized his painting was gone. With wrinkled clothes and uncombed hair, he ran downstairs.

Where are my parents? Flynn thought.

He raced through the kitchen, living room, and dining area. His head was spinning and he had a sinking feeling in his gut. The front door creaked open and his mother stepped into the house holding her purse and car keys.

"You're awake," she said. "Good morning, sweetie."

Without acknowledging her greeting, Flynn said, "Where's my painting? I'm late!"

Georgia held out her hands, palms down, and gestured for him to remain calm.

"It's okay," she said. "Your dad put it in the car already. I was going to let you sleep in. You were up late last night and I thought you needed your rest."

Flynn let out a sigh of relief and relaxed his shoulders.

"I'm going to the college right now to drop it off," his mom said. "I have breakfast in the refrigerator for you. Why don't you stay home and relax."

"I can't," Flynn replied. "I want to see this through."

"Okay," she said, tapping her watch. "But you don't have time for a shower or anything. Grab your shoes and let's go."

Flynn nodded. He threw on his sneakers and bolted toward the car. His mom hopped into the driver's seat and they took off down the road.

Fidgeting in his seat, Flynn watched the digital clock on the dashboard. He gripped the armrest when they ran into construction on the freeway. The traffic inched forward as the clock ticked over to 11:40 am. Georgia turned off at the Grand River College exit. Flynn tapped his foot on the floorboard as his mom searched for a parking space next to the college. As soon as the car came to a stop, Flynn grabbed his painting and sprinted into the building with minutes to spare.

29

November
Naples, Florida

The familiar smell of the chlorine filled Cordelia's nostrils when she emerged from the locker room. Her coach's eyes widened when she saw Cordelia join the other swimmers for the pre-swim stretches.

Pulling Cordelia aside, Coach Neiman said, "You made it! Usually you have excuses for not showing up at night."

Sheepishly looking at the concrete floor, Cordelia thought, *You wouldn't understand my problems.*

"I need more practice," Cordelia said. "I want to be prepared."

Coach Neiman wore a proud smile.

"And my Grandfather gave me time off from work for practices."

"That's good to hear," Coach Neiman said. "Winning a place on the Olympic team is the first step. Training is a full-time job and you may have to take time off from college."

"I understand," said Cordelia. "I'll schedule afternoon classes next semester. Marcel will do the same so we can attend morning and evening practices. If the schedule becomes too much, then I'll consider cutting out a few classes."

Coach Neiman patted Cordelia's shoulder. "I'm so glad to see you're taking this seriously. Being on the Olympic team is a big commitment."

Cordelia headed to the end of the pool with the other swimmers. Her teammates smiled and offered Cordelia hearty congratulations.

I have a shot at a medal! Cordelia thought as she dove into the pool.

∼

Cordelia sat at the kitchen table eating dinner in her grandfather's house. Sometimes she missed having her own space, but the hurricane had damaged her trailer. Now that she could sleep in a bed rather than her aquarium, it made sense to move into the upstairs bedroom. And her grandfather liked the company, at least on most days.

Albert came into the kitchen and sat across from her.

"You needed to talk to me?" he asked with a furrowed brow and crossed arms.

Cordelia set down her sandwich, chewed quickly, and swallowed. She took a big gulp of air, unsure of how to approach the topic of college.

"Yeah," Cordelia said. "Thank you for adjusting my circus performance schedule."

"You're welcome," Albert said with a smile.

"But I need to adjust my college classes, too," Cordelia continued.

His smile quickly faded.

"I talked with Coach today," Cordelia said. "He thinks I should spend more time training. But some of my classes aren't available during my free time after practice."

Albert lowered his eyes and his shoulders slumped. "Are you thinking of taking a semester off? It's hard to get back into the rhythm if you do that. I'm just worried one semester could turn into two…"

Cordelia shook her head. "No, I'm not taking time off. I'll go part-time."

Leaning forward, Albert dropped his elbows onto the table,

rested his chin on his knuckles, and let out a sigh.

"Well," he said. "Your degree will take a lot longer to complete. Your dad never finished his degree."

Cordelia sighed and her shoulder's tensed.

"I know," she said. "But that's a sacrifice I'm willing to make."

"All right, I'll support you on whatever you decide."

She stood, walked over to the other side of table, and gave him a hug. "Thank you, Grandpa."

~

Naples, Florida

Beep, beep, beep!

Cordelia pried her eyes open, rolled over in bed, and stared at the alarm clock. The digital red letters flashed: 5 am.

No sane person should be up this early, she thought.

She rubbed her sleepy eyes, groaned, and thought about the grueling training schedule that lay ahead of her. She trudged into the kitchen and reached into the fruit bowl for a banana. She grabbed a bowl, poured milk into it, added cereal, and sliced the banana on top.

Marcel emerged from his rented quest room. Usually he ate alone, giving Cordelia family time with her grandfather. For the most part, he kept to himself. Her grandfather had made the rules clear, especially when she'd moved into the house from her trailer.

Marcel stretched his arms and yawned. He slowly blinked and wandered around the kitchen.

Normally her grandfather joined her for breakfast, but he had taken the circus out of town for a performance.

"Good morning," Marcel said.

"Morning."

Looking at her breakfast, he said, "Looks pretty good, can I have some, too?"

"Sure," she replied, pointing to the cupboard.

"Coach has me on a new diet: Fruit, vegetables, and lean meat."

"Me too," she replied. "What's your new practice schedule?"

"I have to be in the gym and ready to workout by 6:30."

"That's good," she said. "We can still ride together."

"Not much free time for dating," he added.

"Never seems to be," she said with a weary smile.

Marcel chuckled. "Nope. We've been through a lot together. I guess we can get through this part of the training, right?"

"Yes, definitely," Cordelia said, "You better eat fast or we'll be late for practice."

She finished her cereal and put her bowl in the sink to wash later. She gathered her things and went outside to wait for Marcel.

～

The surface of the pool was flat like a sheet of glass. Bright lights shined high above the empty pool and the room was silent. Cordelia didn't know what to expect on her first full day of Olympic training.

The door of the locker room creaked open, breaking the silence. Coach Neiman's footsteps clicked on the concrete floor, making Cordelia feel a little less lonely. She had practiced in this pool many times, but today everything felt different— almost too real.

"Good morning," Coach Neiman said.

"Morning. Thanks for coming early."

"You're welcome," Coach Neiman said.

Her coach handed Cordelia a copy of her new training routine. She bit her bottom lip and read through the list. She had warm up, a two-hour swim session, time for a snack, an hour and half in the gym, time for a protein shake then a nap, practice jumping off the diving block, muscle warm up, evening swim, and then stretching with yoga. Her coach added a few lunch and dinner suggestions like toast, avocado, eggs, and wrap sandwiches with lean meat and vegetables.

Following her dreams meant making sacrifices. But now, it was all overwhelming. Cordelia's shoulders tensed. Running through the hours of the day in her mind, she calculated how much time she had to relax and do her homework. She would have to go to bed early if she wanted enough time for sleep before getting up at 5 am again.

Marcel will be my workout partner. We'll keep each other motivated, she thought.

30

April 10
Grand River Art and Music College Banquet Hall, Michigan

Students and parents mingled throughout the large art gallery. They were admiring the paintings, photography and the sculptures in the open area. A mix of songs, recorded by students for the competitions, pumped through the overheard speakers.

Outside the gallery in another room was a large stage, where tables and chairs had been set up for the reception dinner. A microphone, drums, guitars, and a keyboard sat on the stage.

Flynn's parents stood next to a painting of a small sailboat on the ocean during a big storm. The mast was broken and a young man with tattered clothing was desperately clinging to the side of the boat. Below the waves was a dark ocean with a mermaid surrounded by blood-thirsty sharks.

Professor Copley pulled a pair of round glasses from his tweed jacket and put them on to examine Flynn's work.

"Great job," Professor Copley said. "I love the mermaid. Where did you get your inspiration for the painting?"

"An artist never gives up their secrets," Flynn said with a sly smile.

The professor chuckled and asked, "Can you at least tell me what it all means?"

"Well," Flynn said, rubbing his chin. "The boy in the boat is crossing the dark stormy waters of human nature and he knows all about loneliness. The boat without a rudder and the sharks represent the world, which remains out of his control. His troubles were blown out to sea by a hurricane. He faced his fears and survived. Rescued by a mermaid, he returned home to be with his friends and family."

"Wow," Professor Copley replied, nodding. "Well, I have to go checkout other entrants. It was good seeing you again." After shaking Flynn's hand, the professor disappeared into the crowd.

Bright lights lit the stage as an emcee stood at the front of the hall and turned on the microphone. "Welcome everyone! You've had the pleasure of seeing some of our paintings and photos, now we're going to share the best of our musical entries. Please give a warm welcome to The Pop Rocks from Whitehall High School, performing a song by Rena Gainsborough."

Three students, including Rena, walked onto the stage. She sat behind her drum kit. Flynn knew Sarah, on the microphone, and the boy on the guitar looked familiar, but he didn't know his name.

"I don't want to miss this," Flynn said to his parents.

They worked their way closer to the stage as the music started. The group's performance had gotten even better from the first time Flynn heard the song. And Vinnie wasn't there to ruin the day.

Sarah's voice started soft and wispy accompanied by a soft guitar line. Halfway through the first verse it picked up when Rena joined with her drums. Soon everyone was tapping their feet to the catchy beat. A few couples even began dancing on the nearby dance floor. Rena's cheeks glowed and her drum kit sparkled under the flashing spotlights.

When they were finished with the song, the band went backstage and another student band took their place. After the last of the four bands had finished, Flynn spotted Rena, her twin sister Deana, and their parents seated at a table in the back of the room. The lights on the stage dimmed and the attendees made their way to the open table.

"Can we sit with Rena and her family?" Flynn asked.

"Sure," Ray said.

Flynn and his parents weaved through the maze of tables and

joined Rena and her family.

"I liked your song, Rena," Georgia said, sitting down next to Ray.

Rena grinned. "Thanks. Composing a song all by myself was tough. I spent a few months practicing and putting all the arrangements together with my friends. I'm nervous playing it in front of people."

"You did great," said Flynn.

"Your painting was awesome," Mr. Gainsborough said. "There are so many talented students here tonight. I hope you two will win scholarships. I'll keep my fingers crossed."

Servers dressed in fancy black outfits filtered through the tables with giant trays, delivering food. The aroma of baked chicken and mashed potatoes drifted through the air. Flynn's nervous stomach twisted and turned.

There was a lot of great artwork in the gallery and he wondered, *How am I going to win?*

He tried to pay attention to the conversation at their table, but his gaze kept drifting to the stage. The lights brightened. The musical instruments were cleared away and replaced with chairs and a long table draped with a black tablecloth. Moments later, Professor Copley and three other teachers walked onto the stage and sat down.

I didn't know he was going to be one of the judges, Flynn thought as a knot formed in his stomach.

Rena reached over, grabbed Flynn's hand, and said, "This is it."

Everyone shifted in their chairs and the clinking of silverware fell silent. The emcee came back out and introduced the judges.

Each professor talked for a couple minutes, explaining their judging process, how long they'd been with the college, and a little about his or her department. The woman in a yellow dress from the music department went last.

"There were so many wonderful entries this year. Everyone should be proud of your accomplishments. I wish we could give everyone a scholarship," the music professor said. "Without further ado, I would like to announce the winner of this year's musical scholarship."

With trembling hands, Rena gripped Flynn's hand.

Peering into the crowd, the music professor said, "Rena Gainsborough, could you please come up to the stage?"

"Congratulations," Flynn's said, rubbing Rena's shoulder.

She gave him a coy smile and said, "Thank you."

Her mother and dad stood and gave Rena a hug. She hurried to the stage, and accepted her certificate as the crowd clapped. Still glowing, Rena shook the judge's hands and then returned to the table.

The room hushed as a judge awarded the scholarship for the sculpture division. Next, the photography department gave out their scholarship.

When the emcee handed the microphone to Professor Copley, Flynn's heart started to pound, his hands became sweaty, and his shoulders were tense.

"While I was very impressed with all of your work, one painting in particular stood out. This year, I am happy to award the art scholarship to: Flynn Parkes."

Flynn's father patted him on the shoulder. Flynn paused a moment to hug his mother and then Rena. Beaming with pride, he floated to the stage bathed in applause.

By the time he returned to the table, everything was a blur.

∼

The caterers cleared the tables and the janitors moved tables and chairs, making room for a small dance floor. Deana stood next to Flynn while her parents gushed over Rena and her scholarship.

"Your painting was okay," Deana said half-heartedly to Flynn.

He wasn't sure it was a compliment or insult.

"Um, thanks," Flynn replied. "Rena's song was great, wasn't it?"

Glancing around the room, Deana stood stiffly in a lavender dress and smoothed her long black hair back over her shoulders. "I suppose so, yeah."

Flynn followed her gaze across the music and art kids. A few of the students had rainbow-colored hair. There was a wide variety of hair styles, piercings, and eclectic clothing. Some were dressed in all black. For once, he didn't feel out of place. He looked forward to four years at the college.

Deana turned up her nose at the milling students. "You know artists don't make any money. You probably won't even get a job."

Flynn rolled his eyes. Before he could enjoy himself, he'd have to get through a two more years of high school filled with "Deanas."

A band of college students stepped onto the stage and started tuning their instruments. The lights dimmed and the band began playing a slow song. People filtered onto the dance floor. Flynn moved away from Deana and headed toward Rena.

He extended his hand and asked, "Would you like to dance?"

Rena glanced at her parents. Her dad nodded.

Flynn and Rena stepped onto the dance floor. Flynn rested his hands on Rena's hips as she leaned in close to his ear.

Flynn took a deep breath, let it out slowly, and asked, "Can we go out again?"

"I thought you'd never ask." Rena said with a coy smile. "I'd like that."

Everything fell into place, Flynn thought. *I have a scholarship and a girl who likes me.*

They glided across the dance floor.

31

May 4
Naples, Florida

Knock! Knock! Knock!
"Come in," Cordelia said

Her grandpa entered her bedroom with a handful of mail, sat down on the edge of her bed, and handed her a letter.

"This came for you today," Albert whispered. "It's from your dad."

Her fingers trembled. She opened the envelope and read the letter:

Dear Cordelia,

Congratulations on landing a spot on the Olympic Swim team! I'm so proud of you! I'm sorry I wasn't there for your accomplishment. Your mom and I were there in spirit.

I'm so sorry for hurting you. My only wish is to see you succeed and be happy. I'll do everything in my power to make it up to you, I promise.

Tell Albert thank you for finding the evidence that will help my case. Hopefully, the judge will reduce my sentence. My court date is May 18 and I was hoping you would come to my hearing. I could use your support.

Love,
Dad

Cordelia dropped her hands to her side.

"What did he say?" Albert asked.

"He asked if we could go to his court hearing."

Albert sighed. "How do you feel about going? Do you want to be there?"

Cordelia searched her feelings. Slowly, she was letting her heart mend.

"Yes," she said after a long pause. "We should go."

"I'll book us some plane tickets."

Warmth washed over Cordelia. She'd been scattered and stretched thin for so long, but now all the pieces of her life were falling into place. Her hard work and patience were paying off. She was going to the Olympics and her father might even be there.

I hope the evidence is enough to free him, she worried.

∼

May 18
District Court, Siren Bay, Michigan

"Relax," Albert said, tapping Cordelia's jiggling knee.

They sat in the front row of the spectator area in the courtroom.

She sighed, sat up straight, and suppressed her nervous energy.

Salvatore, dressed in a blue jumpsuit, sat stiff-backed next to his attorney, Mr. Brodie. The ledger and contracts were neatly stacked on the table.

Mr. Brodie turned around in his seat, looked at Albert, and whispered, "The judge will decide whether or not to review the new evidence. He won't make an immediate judgment."

Cordelia kept her fingers crossed for a positive outcome.

Two bailiffs solemnly stood next to the judge's bench, their gazes sweeping over the courtroom. The jury box remained empty.

"All rise for the Honorable Judge Robleson," the bailiff announced.

Everyone stood as the judge came into the room and sat down behind the bench.

"You can be seated," Judge Robleson spoke into his microphone.

After a few moments, the judge called Mr. Brodie to discuss Salvatore's case. Mr. Brodie stood and paced in front of the bench. The judge's smile turned into a scowl when he glanced over at Cordelia's father.

Albert leaned over and put his arm around her shoulder.

"Your Honor," Mr. Brodie began. "Today I bring a ledger, contracts, and a business plan written by Jack Weston. This new evidence will show that Mr. Weston should bear the weight of the charges brought against my client. This evidence will show that my client wasn't the mastermind behind the crimes, only an accomplice. My client admits his wrongdoing and he has seen the error of his ways. However, we're seeking to reduce his sentence or grant him consideration for early parole."

One of the bailiffs stepped forward to retrieve the documents from the table and delivered the paperwork to the judge.

With his bifocals perched on end of his nose, the judge flipped through a few pages. The judge stopped reviewing the papers, peered over the top of his glasses, and glared at Salvatore.

Cordelia held her breath.

Looking back at Mr. Brodie, the judge said, "I need time to review the new evidence. We'll meet back here in two weeks."

The judge and Salvatore's attorney conversed back and forth, but Cordelia's mind was buzzing too much to pay attention. She had her heart set on hearing good news.

"Another two weeks?" she whispered to Albert.

"There's a lot to look at," he said.

Carrying the evidence in his hand, the judge stood, left the bench, and stepped out of the back door of the courtroom.

"I know. I had hope…" Cordelia replied.

Her father turned and gave her a weary smile as the bailiffs led him away.

June 1
District Court, Siren Bay Michigan

The bailiff walked into the courtroom and announced, "All rise for the Honorable Judge Robleson."

The judge's black robes swished as he came into the courtroom and sat behind his bench.

"Please be seated."

Albert and Cordelia sat behind Salvatore and his attorney.

Reading from his notes, the judge directed his statements toward Salvatore.

"After reviewing the new evidence, the court has determined a reduced sentence is in order. Salvatore Da Vinci's 10-year sentence will be reduced to five."

Salvatore placed his hands together and raised them to his lips. He began to tremble as his attorney patted him on the back.

Cordelia had the urge to jump up and celebrate, but she kept her composure. She hugged Albert instead.

"We did it," her grandpa whispered in her ear.

Holding back her tears, she nodded. Salvatore stood and turned long enough to mouth "thank you" to Cordelia before being led out of the courtroom by the bailiff.

Mr. Brodie packed his briefcase and came over to where Cordelia and Albert sat.

"Congratulations," Mr. Brodie said, shaking their hands. "That evidence certainly helped."

"Now what?" Albert asked.

"I'll fill out the necessary paperwork and then the judge will sign off on it." Looking at Cordelia, Mr. Brodie continued, "Your dad will be eligible for parole in three years."

Cordelia leaned back and stared into space. *Three years? That's a long time!* she thought. *Will he be out before the Olympics?*

32

3 years later, June
Grand River Art and Music College

The TV screen flashed all different colors and the speakers blared car revving noises. Boxes of half-packed belongings lay scattered around the dorm room. Flynn sat on the end of his bed with his game controller in his hands.

"I can't believe the first year of college is over already," Flynn said.

Rena lounged in the beanbag chair with her feet propped up on a crate. She looked comfortable playing the video game.

"Yeah," Rena said. "Me, too."

Her red Ferrari whizzed past Flynn's blue Lamborghini and crossed the finish line.

"Darn it," Flynn said. "You beat me again!"

Rena laughed.

Flynn's drawings on the walls fluttered as the dorm room door opened and his roommate walked in.

Alex waved with his free hand. "Hey guys."

"You want to play?" Rena asked. "I've got an hour left before my parents will be here to load up my stuff. That's plenty of time to beat you both."

Alex chuckled. "Nah, watching you beat Flynn is enough entertainment for me. Besides, I gotta go through all this mail. My charming roommate forgot to pick it up last week so there's a ton."

He sifted through the envelopes. "At least this one doesn't look like a bill for next semester." Alex held out a large tan envelope.

Flynn's face turned pale. He set his controller down and ripped open the envelope. Rena watched him, curiosity plain on her face. Two airplane tickets, a letter, several brochures, and a business card fell out of the envelope.

Flynn picked up the letter and read it. The sound of the video game and the room faded away. He heard the lions roaring on the beach, he felt the heat of the fire, and the images of the circus consumed his thoughts.

Dear Flynn,

You probably thought that you'd never hear from me again, but I think you're going to be happy you opened this letter.

I hope college is going well for you and Rena. I'm sure you're doing great things. I hope you're using your powers responsibly.

After years of hard work, I'm proud to announce Cordelia and Marcel will be competing in the Summer Olympics in Atlanta, Georgia this July. Your bravery saved the circus and your actions helped Cordelia and Marcel achieve dreams. We'd be honored if you and Rena would join us at the Olympics.

I included in the package the schedule of events, hotel reservations, airplane tickets, and my phone number.

Talk to you soon
Albert Da Vinci

"Who's it from?" Rena asked.

Flynn stared off into space.

Rena set her controller down and pried herself from the bean bag. "Flynn?"

Holding up two plane tickets, he grinned. "It's been awhile, but are you up for another adventure?"

"What are you talking about?" Rena asked, looking closer at the destination. "Plane tickets for Atlanta, Georgia?"

"Albert invited us to the Summer Olympics," Flynn said, still in disbelief.

Rena squealed and jumped up and down.

"Man, your summer sounds more exciting than mine," Alex said, holding up a letter of his own. "The most exciting thing I got was a summer internship offer. You win."

"That's great," said Flynn. "You should take the internship. We'll all meet back here next September to catch up."

"Okay, sounds like a plan." Alex pointed to the boxes strewn around the room. "Start packing. We need to be out of the dorm by tomorrow."

"I'll help," Rena offered.

Flynn packed his things and dreamed of the summer ahead.

33

I hope I packed enough for two weeks, Cordelia thought.

The bed of Albert's pickup truck was piled high with three suitcases and a cooler. Humidity hung in the air, predicting an early morning rain. Marcel covered the suitcases with a tarp and strapped everything down with bungee cords.

"Are you forgetting anything?" Albert asked.

Cordelia thought for a moment before responding. "No, I don't think so."

Turning to Marcel, Albert said, "Keep Cordelia safe."

"Yes, sir," Marcel said, shaking Albert's hand.

Marcel jumped into the driver's seat of the truck and gave Cordelia and Albert some privacy.

"I wish you were coming with us," Cordelia said, giving her grandpa a hug.

"Me too," Albert replied. "But your dad's release date is delayed."

"I know, but I'm worried you'll miss my event."

Albert sighed. "Someone needs to be there for him when he gets out. All he has is the shirt on his back. No one else wants to pick him up."

Cordelia bit her bottom lip and looked at Marcel. From behind the window, he gave her a sheepish grin. She felt less angry toward her dad and time was slowly healing her wounds.

"I promise we'll be there on time," Albert said.

Cordelia hugged him again and hopped into the passenger seat of the truck. She waved goodbye and her smile faded as Marcel pulled out of the driveway. She quietly stared out the window.

"Are you okay?" Marcel asked.

"I'm worried they won't be there."

He squeezed her hand. "They'll be there."

Giving him a half smile, she tapped her foot on the floorboards.

"Albert will do everything in his power to be there," Marcel reassured her.

Nodding, she tried relaxing her shoulders on the long drive to Atlanta.

~

July 19
Atlanta, Georgia

Flynn yawned as he knocked on Rena's hotel room door.

"Are you ready?" he called out.

Rena opened the door, wiping the sleep from her eyes. "Yep," she said with a smirk. "What's the plan?"

"I talked to Albert on the phone. He said Cordelia and Marcel would meet us in the lobby at 10 am." Flynn said.

Rena checked her watch. "Then we better get moving."

She closed her door, slipped the key into her pocket, and they took the elevator down to the lobby. They found a pair of comfortable chairs nestled between large potted plants and sat down. Newspapers were scattered on a coffee table with all the headlines focusing on the Olympics.

"I can't believe we're really here," Rena said with wide eyes.

"Me either," Flynn said. "We get to see the Olympics in person instead of on TV. How cool is that?"

"Very!" Rena pointed to the open elevator and waved. "They're here."

Marcel and Cordelia weaved through the chattering people in

the lobby and joined Flynn and Rena.

"When did you guys get here?" Rena asked.

"Two days ago," Cordelia said. "We had a lot to go over with our coaches."

"We got here late last night," Flynn said. "Where's Albert?"

With slumped shoulders, Cordelia's face turned pale. She looked down at the carpet floor and sighed.

"He's coming," Marcel said.

Marcel and Cordelia sat in the chairs on the other side of the coffee table.

"Albert is picking up Salvatore from prison first," Marcel said. He took Cordelia's hand and squeezed it.

"Salvatore?" Flynn shivered. "I thought I would never see him again."

"He's changed," Cordelia whispered, giving them a hopeful smile. "After he lost his powers, his empathy returned. Now, he regrets everything."

"It wasn't all his fault," Marcel added.

Cordelia cast him a grateful smile.

"Jack had his own plans for the future of the circus and the scroll," Marcel continued. "We stopped him before it was too late."

Flynn nodded. He knew Cordelia should forgive her father. Time would tell whether Salvatore had changed or not.

"When are your competitions?" Rena asked.

Marcel handed her a brochure. "Here's the event schedule with all the times and locations. I circled our events."

Rena glanced over the brochure and then passed it to Flynn.

"Thanks," Flynn said. "It'll be fun to watch."

"If you need to get anywhere, for an event or to a restaurant, there's a shuttle service and taxi that stops in front of the hotel every half hour," Cordelia said.

"Great," Rena said.

Flynn skimmed over the schedule, noting the circled events. "Marcel, it looks like you're up first tomorrow afternoon."

"Yeah," Marcel said. "Cordelia has her first one tomorrow night."

"At night? Thank goodness you found the ribbon," Rena said.

"Yeah," Cordelia said. "I never thought I'd be so happy to sleep in a regular bed."

"Do you still…" Flynn cautiously asked. "Turn into a mermaid?"

"Sometimes," Cordelia said bashfully. "Only when I want to."

"We're going to check out some competitions," Marcel said. "Want to join us?"

With a wide grin, Flynn glanced at Rena.

"Heck yeah!" Rena nodded enthusiastically.

34

Flynn saw Cordelia walking in front of the bleachers, peering up at the crowd. Her white jumpsuit had red stripes across the shoulder and her sneakers were decorated with the USA team logo. From the pinched look on her face, he guessed Albert and Salvatore hadn't arrived yet.

"I feel bad for her," Rena whispered. "To get all the way here and not have her family to cheer her on."

"We'll do the cheering for them," Flynn said. He stood and waved until Cordelia spotted him. She worked her way up to the seat they had saved for her.

"Is Marcel nervous?" Rena asked.

"Definitely," Cordelia said. "We're both nervous. My event isn't for four hours and I'm still freaking out. A lot of pressure."

Rena patted Cordelia on the back and said, "You'll both do great."

"Thanks." Cordelia smiled.

Flynn noticed how much Cordelia had changed. When he met her, she had a world of sorrow and anger behind her smile, but now she had a confident gleam in her eye. Her back was straight and her head held high as if she'd been born for this competition.

An hour passed and several competitions were completed.

How can one person lift so much weight? Flynn wondered, anxiously waiting for Marcel's turn.

Marcel sat on the bench with the USA team coach beside him.

They were speaking to one another, but Flynn couldn't tell what they were saying. Marcel's face turned pale when the large man from the Swedish team picked up the bar like it was nothing, held it steady, and then dropped the weight in one smooth motion. The sound echoed through the auditorium.

The announcer spoke over the loud speaker, "Our final competitor in the 105kg weightlifting event is Marcel Duchamp. If Marcel is successful, he'll move to the next phase of the competition."

Flynn leaned forward. Cordelia clasped her hands in front of her mouth.

Marcel stepped up to the chalk box, applied chalk to his hands, and clapped them together before taking his place in front of the giant barbell. He closed his eyes for a moment and then positioned his feet shoulder-width apart. Squatting, he picked up the barbell and paused when he stood. He inhaled deeply, then exhaled and flipped the bar up by his shoulders.

Rena grabbed Flynn's hand and squeezed. Flynn grinned, but kept his gaze locked on the ring below.

Marcel kicked one foot back, inhaled, pointed his elbows forward, and as he exhaled, he pushed the barbell over his head.

When the judge nodded, he dropped the weight to the floor. It bounced once and rolled to a stop a second later.

Cordelia threw her fist in the air and cheered, "He did it!"

The audience shot to their feet and clapped. The coach patted Marcel on the back. Marcel seemed distracted from whatever the coach was saying, too busy scanning the stands. Flynn knew the moment he'd spotted them, because he grinned widely.

"I hope he holds out against the Swedish weightlifter," Rena said.

"He will," Cordelia said. "And he won't even need his powers. He trained hard for this."

"He'll do great," Flynn chimed in.

Cordelia rubbed her neck and then her face turned pale.

"What's wrong?" Flynn asked.

"Darn it! I can't be here for the final round," Cordelia said. "I'm running late and I forgot my locket. I must've left it in my gym bag in the locker. I'm going to get it and then I need to warm up before my event."

"We'll stay and wait for Marcel to finish his match," Flynn said. "We'll all be there to watch your competition."

Cordelia's smile faltered. "I hope so."

~

Cordelia stomped back and forth across the floor in the empty locker room. With red cheeks and trembling hands, she rubbed her purple gold locket with her thumbs. Her shoulders were tense and nerves frayed.

Where are Dad and Grandpa? she wondered. *They're supposed to be here by now. They're going to miss my event!*

Cordelia stopped in her tracks when the lid on the locket popped open and the overhead lights dimmed. Several tiny purple orbs floated out of the locket and swirled around Cordelia's body. The orbs slowly dissolved into billowing smoke and then formed into a ghostly image of Cordelia's mom. Her mother's presence felt like a warm hug.

"Mom, I'm worried. Dad and Grandpa aren't going make it!"

"Everything will be all right," Gala whispered.

"I hope so," Cordelia said, fighting back tears.

"I'm so proud of you." Gala kissed Cordelia on the cheek and vanished.

With a heavy heart, Cordelia fastened the locket around her neck and walked out of the locker room.

35

Staring at her feet, Cordelia shuffled down the hallway toward the pool auditorium. She passed by a few athletes in the corridor and the muffled cheers of the audience grew louder. The faint sound of her name echoed off the tiled walls.

Mom, is that you? she wondered.

She lifted her head and her heart filled with joy when she saw Albert and Salvatore running down the hall. She ran into her father's arms and gave him a giant hug.

"You made it!" Cordelia said.

"I'm missed you so much," Salvatore said, rocking her back and forth.

After searching her heart, Cordelia answered honestly, "Me, too."

"We're here with minutes to spare!" Albert said.

"We drove straight to the hotel so I could change," Salvatore said, letting go from their embrace. "We got here as soon as we could."

Albert held the schedule up and said, "They gave us this brochure on the hotel shuttle bus. We ran around the complex looking for you."

"I'm so glad you found me," Cordelia said. "I'm so happy you're here! I thought you would never make it."

Albert and Salvatore were beaming with pride.

"I wouldn't miss this for the world," Salvatore said.

A warm feeling of relief washed over Cordelia's body.

"You missed Marcel's event earlier," Cordelia said. "I didn't get to see the end."

"Oh no!" Albert groaned. He shook his fist. "I really wanted to see him compete. I hope he won."

"Me too," Cordelia nodded. "Flynn and Rena are here, too. They're in the bleachers somewhere. Maybe you can sit with them."

Kissing her forehead, Albert said, "Okay, we'll find them. Good luck!"

Tapping his wrist watch, Salvatore said, "According to the schedule, you're up in half an hour. You better get going."

"Thanks," Cordelia said, giving them one last hug.

With a renewed sense of peace, she sprinted toward the pool auditorium.

∼

Spectators packed the bleachers and the athletes lined up on the back side of the pool. Swimmers were stretching and talking with their coaches. Flynn looked at the clock on the wall: 6:30 pm.

The hair on the back of Flynn's neck stood on end when he saw Albert and Salvatore climbing up the bleachers toward them. Unable to move a muscle, flashbacks flooded Flynn's mind. He remembered the melting pocket watch, the roar of the lions, and Salvatore's thin black mustache that curled at the ends.

"He's here," Marcel grunted, raising his bushy eyebrows and clenching his fists.

"Yeah, I see him," Flynn grumbled.

Rena grabbed Flynn's arm and slid closer. None of them stood, waved, or attempted to draw attention in anyway.

Albert waved when he spotted them. With a sigh, Flynn and Rena slid down, making room for two more. Marcel stared down at Cordelia's father. Salvatore came to a halt a foot away and extended his hand.

With a scowl, Marcel looked at Salvatore from head to toe.

Lowering his eyes, Salvatore said, "I know I messed up, but I'm a changed man and I paid my dues."

Marcel's muscles bulged underneath his t-shirt and his chiseled jaw quivered.

Oh no! Flynn thought.

"I promise, I'll make it up to you. All of you." Salvatore's gaze paused on each one of them.

"Let's put our differences aside for a moment and support Cordelia," Albert stepped in. "We can sort this all out later, okay?"

Marcel reached out and aggressively shook Salvatore's hand. Salvatore's knees slightly buckled and he grimaced a little.

"You're right, Albert." Marcel sighed. He let go of Salvatore's hand and sat back down. "We're here for Cordelia."

Wow! Flynn's jaw dropped and his shoulders relaxed. *Marcel has changed.*

Albert scooted past Marcel and sat next to Flynn. Salvatore took a seat at the end.

Flynn ignored Salvatore and watched the swimmers warm up instead.

"Sorry I missed your first event, Marcel," Albert tried to change the subject. "How did you do?"

Marcel was slow in answering, his jaw was still clenched and his eyes looked straightforward. Flynn leaned over to Albert, hoping to talk over the loud voices of the audience.

"He took first place," Flynn said. "You should've seen the Swedish guy he went against at the end. He was huge."

Albert gasped, turned to Marcel, and said, "A first place gold medal? That's amazing. Congratulations, Marcel!"

Albert patted Marcel on the shoulder.

"I owe you a lot," Marcel said with a huge smile. "Giving me a place to stay and helping me find a coach. Thank you."

"You're welcome," Albert said.

Leaning forward, Salvatore said, "That's great. Congratulations."

Marcel gave Salvatore a quick nod and then his gaze darted to the swimming pool.

Hoping the tension in the air would break, Flynn scanned the line of athletes.

"There she is," Flynn said, pointing to Cordelia.

The swimmers lined up for the competition. Cordelia, in her blue one-piece suit, adjusted her goggles and shook out her arms.

As the announcer's voice came over the speakers, the crowd quieted. Flynn leaned forward with anticipation.

∼

Looking over the crowd, Cordelia saw Albert and Salvatore sitting in the bleachers. She let out a sigh of relief.

I hope things are going back to normal, she thought, feeling the presence of her mom.

Adjusting her goggles, Cordelia stood on the diving block waiting for the starter signal. She cleared her mind and focused all her energy on the pool.

BEEP!

With perfect form, she dove into the pool with her hands above her head in a streamlined position. Bending her knees, she flexed her hips and thighs to cut through the water as if she had her mermaid tail. Rotating her body to the surface, she inhaled through her mouth. In a matter of seconds, she reached the end of the 50-meter pool. She flipped her body with a somersault underwater and used both legs to propel off the pool wall for the final lap.

The seconds flew by in a blur. When her fingertips touched the opposite end of the pool, she popped her head above the water and took a deep breath. The audience cheered as she pushed her goggles up onto her forehead. Glancing at the time clock, she burst into tears; her time had just broken the women's world record. She raised her fist in victory and her eyes toward her family.

∼

Savoring the moment, Cordelia stood on the top tier of the platform with the Olympic flag draped on the wall behind her. A pendant with the American flag was pinned to her jacket. She scanned the bleachers and found her father and grandpa standing proud. Marcel wore a giant grin. Flynn and Rena stood beside him, smiling.

"And the gold medal goes to Cordelia Da Vinci, Team USA," the announcer said over a loud speaker.

The Olympic official draped the gold medal around Cordelia's neck. With a wide smile, she shook his hand. She raised her fists in the air as the crowd cheered. She picked up the gold medal, raised it to her lips, and kissed it while tears streamed down her cheeks.

All my dreams came true! she thought, beaming with pride.

36

Two weeks later
Whitehall, Michigan

Rena's car pulled into the driveway of the L.C. Woodruff Inn. A weathered brick exterior and a steep gabled roof made the old building look tall. A large picture window accentuated the front and a bay window was centered on the west wall.

"We're here," Rena said, parking her car in front of the building.

A large sign on the front lawn read "Party for the Olympic Gold Medal Winners."

"Where is everybody?" Rena asked

"We're early, but Albert should be here with the caterers," Flynn replied.

"Where do we unload the equipment?" Rena asked.

"I think Albert wants us to set up on the balcony," Flynn said pointing to the back of the Inn that faced Lake Michigan. "Let's find out."

Flynn grabbed the speakers and Rena carried the round cases containing her drums. They made their way inside the Inn to find a smiling middle-aged couple behind the check-in counter.

"Welcome," the man said. "You must be here for the Da Vinci celebration?"

Flynn nodded.

"We bought the Inn a month ago," the woman said. "We've

been busy with renovations and you'll be the first ones to use the remodeled banquet hall! We hope you enjoy it."

"Do you need help bringing the equipment inside?" the man asked, holding out his hands.

"No," Rena replied. "We got it, thanks."

"Where should we set-up?" Flynn asked.

"Albert wanted the band on the balcony," the man said. "I hope that's okay?"

"Yep," Rena said. "That'll work."

"Follow me," the man said, pointing to the staircase on the other side of the lobby.

Flynn and Rena followed the man up to the banquet hall, which was filled with tables and chairs. Two sets of sliding glass doors interrupted the floor-to-ceiling windows that offered an expansive view of Lake Michigan.

They went through one of the sliding doors to the large balcony where the deck was furnished with a small stage and dance floor. A few tables and chairs were shaded by sandy brown umbrellas.

Flynn and Rena looked out over Lake Michigan. Rolling waves crashed on the beach and the seagulls squawked as they circled overhead.

"It's a great night to be outside," the man said.

"It is," Rena agreed. "Warm weather and a clear sky to see the stars."

"If you need anything, let me know," the man said. "I'll leave you two alone to set up,"

"Thanks," Flynn said.

Rena and Flynn went back to the car for the rest of the instruments. Once they had the keyboard and speakers set up, Flynn stepped back and wiped his brow.

"Darn it," Flynn grunted. "I forgot something. I'll be right back."

Flynn slipped back down to the car and grabbed a violin case and his art supplies. Instead of going through the Inn, he took a shortcut. He walked around to the back of the building, and climbed up a wooden stairway leading to the balcony. When he reached the top of the steps, Rena gave him a curious look.

"Violin case and a sketch pad?" Rena asked.

"The violin belongs to my dad," Flynn said. "I snuck it out of the house this morning. I'm hoping my dad will play a few songs tonight."

"Does he know you took it?" Rena asked, rubbing her forehead.

Flynn hid the violin case behind Rena's drum kit and chuckled. "No, it's a surprise."

"And the sketch pad?" Rena asked. "Are you expecting trouble?"

Before Flynn could the answer the question, Albert and Cordelia emerged from the Inn and stepped onto the balcony. Albert's face lit up and a smile spread across his face. He shook Flynn's hand and gave Rena a hug with one arm. Underneath his other elbow, Albert carried a dark green ammo box.

"I'm so glad you could make it," Albert said with watery eyes. "I don't know where the circus would be without your help."

"You've changed our lives," Flynn said. "We wouldn't miss this party for the world."

Flynn heard some footsteps and he felt a tap on his shoulder. He turned around and the hair on the back of his neck stood on end when he found himself staring eye-to-eye with Salvatore. In a state of shock, Flynn heard the imaginary roar of a lion echo in his ears.

"Flynn," Albert said. "Before all the guests arrive, could you help us one last time?"

"Sure," Flynn stammered, feeling a little awkward. "What do you need me to do?"

Salvatore reached into his pocket a pulled out the watch.

Flynn's jaw dropped and a bead of sweat formed on his brow.

With desperation in his eyes, Flynn said, "Albert, why didn't you destroy it?"

"We need it for one last thing," Albert said. "We're going to save Cordelia's mom from dying in that car accident."

"I'll go back in time with the watch," Salvatore said. "Just before the crash, I'll stop time and pull my wife out of the car."

Looking at Cordelia, Salvatore said, "Do you want me to pull you out of the accident, too?"

Albert wrung his hands and tapped his foot.

"That would change the whole outcome of things," Flynn said.

Salvatore nodded. "It could cause a ripple in time, having drastic effects on our lives. But it's up to Cordelia."

Looking down at the scars on her legs, Cordelia thought back on all the pain she had gone through and somehow survived. She felt stronger, more resilient, and independent. She could take on the world.

"No," Cordelia whispered. "The past changed my life, but it also made me who I am today."

Albert gave her a warm smile and asked, "Are you sure?"

All the events that led up to this day changed everyone's lives. Cordelia didn't want to be selfish and change the course of history for everyone, better or worse.

She thought about how changing the past would affect Flynn. *He wouldn't have his powers.*

"Yes, I'm sure," Cordelia said. "We would've never met Flynn and he wouldn't be able to create his wonderful drawings."

"Thanks," Flynn said, blushing. "Things would be a lot different."

Looking at Salvatore, Albert asked, "Are you ready to do this?"

Salvatore hesitated for a moment before nodding. He held the pocket watch in the palm of his hand. Albert set the ammo box on the table and popped open the top. Albert reached inside and pulled out the Secret Talent Scroll.

Feeling anxious, Flynn listened to Albert read the spell.

"I call upon the four classical elements: Wind, fire, earth, and water," Albert said. "Wind moves sand. Fire creates earth and ash. Earth absorbs water. Water quenches fire. Give Salvatore the power to control space and time with his pocket watch."

Beach sand kicked up into the air, blew over a candle flame, and exploded into a small firework show. A wave crashed on the beach and a spout of water leapt in the air. The water sailed over to the deck and extinguished the firework sparks. The ashes sprinkled over Salvatore's hand.

"And now for the second spell," Albert said.

Albert reached inside the ammo box, pulled out the ribbon, and unrolled it on the table.

In a trance, Salvatore closed his eyes as Albert read the spell.

The gold sheen on the watch brightened and sparkled. The cover opened and a yellowish glow emitted from the edges.

Salvatore's eyelids snapped open. His hand trembled and his knees wobbled.

"I know how to save my wife," Salvatore said.

"Now what," Flynn asked. "What do you need me to do?"

"Could you draw a wormhole?" Salvatore asked.

"A wormhole? What's that? How?"

"Imagine a tunnel through space with two separate ends in time," Salvatore said. "The first point in time is where we stand today. And the other end of the tunnel is six years ago, just before the car accident."

Flynn squinted his eyes as Salvatore described how time warped and wrapped through dark matter. Using Salvatore's description, Flynn imagined what a wormhole would look like.

Flynn tore out two sheets of paper from the sketchpad and sat down at the table. Using the flat edge of the pencil, Flynn created a long spiral out from the center of the pages to the edges. The shaded curves looked like the shell of a snail. He added hundreds of small spheres along the flow of the vortex.

Using his imagination, Salvatore constructed and wrote on a napkin the mathematical formula for creating a tunnel through space and time.

Flynn looked at the equation, scratched his head, and shrugged his shoulders.

"That's beyond me," Flynn mumbled.

Nevertheless, Flynn copied the equation on his drawing. He didn't know what all the numbers and symbols meant, but he was curious to see if Salvatore's theory would work or not.

Flynn set the two sheets of paper on the ground and waited in anticipation. The drawing slowly rippled across the paper. The charcoal grey transformed into blue, white, and yellow. The dark edges turned into the black emptiness of space. Millions of spinning stars streaked in a small spiral. The lights moved faster and faster toward the center of the drawing, creating a hypnotic tunnel.

In awe, Flynn stepped backward.

"I hope this works," Salvatore said. His thin black mustache quivered.

Resting his hand on Salvatore's shoulder, Albert said "You can do it. I believe in you, son."

Salvatore's shoulders and posture straightened. His sullen eyes brightened.

"Thanks Dad," Salvatore whispered.

Albert nodded. "Good luck."

Everyone nervously backed away from the drawing, giving Salvatore plenty of room. Stuffing the watch in his pocket, Salvatore jumped into the hole. A strong gravitational force sucked Salvatore into the vortex and whisked him away. His entire body became a blur, shrinking until he disappeared into the depths of the wormhole.

With eyes wide open, Rena exclaimed under her breath, "Wow!"

37

A low hum emitted from the vortex, growing louder with each passing minute.

"What is that noise?" Cordelia whispered.

Flynn shrugged his shoulders. Albert crossed his arms and rested his chin on his knuckles.

The spiral pulsated and changed colors, varying between blue, purple, and white. The low hum intensified into a screech. Squealing tires, crunching metal, and a loud thud reverberated through the tunnel and echoed over the beach. Everyone covered their ears. Cordelia felt a twinge of pain in her knees.

Holding her breath, Cordelia grabbed Albert's hand and buried her face in his shoulder.

Leaning in for a closer look, Flynn saw a blurry speck grow larger as it neared the lip of the tunnel. The outline of Salvatore's body came into focus and barreled toward them. Startled, Flynn stumbled backwards.

Carrying Gala in his arms, Salvatore emerged from the wormhole. With wobbly knees and trembling arms, he set her down on the ground. She looked around in bewilderment.

Cordelia opened her arms and ran over to her mom. Nearly knocking her down, she gave Gala a giant hug. Tears of joy streamed down Cordelia's cheeks.

"The last thing I remembered is driving to the gym with Cordelia," Gala said, her voice shaken. "How did I get here? And where am I?"

"We have a lot to talk about," Salvatore said.

Salvatore leaned in closer and wrapped his arms around his wife and daughter.

Looking over at Flynn, Salvatore mouthed the words, *Thank you.*

A sense of peace washed over Flynn's heart. A question popped into his mind.

Flynn looked at Cordelia and asked, "If your mom was pulled from the car crash, how did that affect the past?"

"I don't know," Cordelia whispered.

Cordelia closed her eyes and thought about the fateful day after the accident. The old memory of her mom dying melted away and a new memory grew inside her mind. She remembered lying in a hospital bed with her legs wrapped in two white casts. Her dad sat on the floor with his back against the wall. His hair was disheveled and he looked as though he hadn't slept in days.

"What happened?" Cordelia groaned.

Salvatore looked up at her with red and teary eyes, "You've been in a car accident."

Shaking her head in denial, Cordelia and asked, "Where's mom?"

"Your mom…" Salvatore choked up. "Disappeared."

"Disappeared?" Cordelia's eyes widened. "What do you mean?"

"I know. None of this makes any sense," Salvatore said. "Gala wouldn't abandon you at the accident."

Cordelia squirmed uncomfortably in the hospital bed and clenched the blanket with her fist.

"What about the crystal ball?" Cordelia asked with frustration. "It'll tell us where to find mom."

"Your grandpa and I tried that already," Salvatore said "The image inside the crystal ball froze in place. One moment Gala is driving the car, and the next moment she disappeared from the vehicle before impact."

"Why did the crystal ball skip?" Cordelia asked.

"I don't know," Salvatore said.

"What do we do now?" Cordelia asked.

"The police are investigating the accident. They're looking for any clues about her disappearance."

Cordelia's shoulders tightened. She wished should could jump out of bed and search for her mom.

"Where's Grandpa?" Cordelia asked. "Maybe he'll know what to do?"

"He went downstairs to the hospital cafeteria," Salvatore mumbled. "He'll be back later."

Cordelia tilted her head toward the ceiling, clenched her eyes shut, and let out a long breath of air.

"There's something else," Salvatore said.

Cordelia lifted her head off the pillow, looked at her dad, and asked, "What is it?"

"Your grandpa and I used the scroll to give me the power to control space and time," Salvatore said, holding up the pocket watch. "I went back in time!"

"You couldn't find her?" Cordelia asked.

Salvatore looked at Cordelia and said, "I went back a hundred times, but I couldn't find your mom or fix the past."

"But…Why?" Cordelia stammered.

"I tried warning you and your mom but you couldn't see or hear me. The louder I spoke, the farther away you seemed. I couldn't touch or interact with you. I was powerless to stop the accident. I was like a ghost."

"Where did Mom go?"

"I don't know," Salvatore replied in a solemn voice. "In the blink of an eye she vanished from the car just before the accident. It was almost like someone took her."

"Vanished?" Cordelia cried. ""Who took her and how?"

Salvatore shrugged his shoulders. "I don't know. The scroll is worthless if I can't control my powers." He shook his fist. "Why is this happening to me?"

Emotions crashed down upon Cordelia.

With tears streaming down his cheek, Salvatore whispered, "I failed you, your mom, and everyone."

Traveling Circus and the Skeleton Key

He rose to his feet, walked closer to the hospital bed, and held up the pocket watch.

"Dad, what are you doing?" Cordelia asked with fear in her voice.

"I'm lost without your mother. The pain is too great," Salvatore said with quivering lips.

Swinging the watch back and forth, Salvatore whispered, "Time, erase my sadness.... Erase my tears... Erase my grief..."

His brown eyes faded into black coal and his fists clenched. He stumbled forward and collapsed onto his knees.

"Dad!" Cordelia yelled.

She tried getting out of the bed, but the casts kept her planted in the bed. She bent forward and rested her hands on her father's shoulder.

"Are you okay?" she cried.

She felt the warmth of his skin through his clothes turn cold.

"I'm fine," he said, looking up at Cordelia with a dark stare.

He picked himself off the floor and straightened his clothes as though nothing was wrong.

Albert pushed open the door and walked into the hospital room.

"Did I miss something?" Albert asked with a puzzled look on his face.

"I'm leaving Cordelia with you," Salvatore said.

"What do you mean?" Albert said with concern in his voice. "Where are you going? What's going on?"

"Whatever it takes, I'm going to find my wife. I'll search for her until the end of time," Salvatore said.

"What?" Albert raised his voice. "The police are looking for Gala. Maybe she'll come home on her own."

"I can't wait around for the police," Salvatore said.

"When are you coming home?" Cordelia stammered.

"Not until I find her," Salvatore said.

Salvatore burst out of the hospital room and stormed down the hall. Albert chased after him, leaving Cordelia alone.

"Don't go!" Cordelia's heart shattered.

After several minutes, Albert came back into the room and said, "Your dad has changed."

Cordelia's body trembled.

"What happened while I was gone?" Albert asked.

"Dad asked the pocket watch to take away his sadness," Cordelia whimpered.

Albert leaned over the bed and hugged Cordelia. She buried her head in his arms and cried.

"He must've erased his ability to feel empathy," Albert whispered.

Cordelia opened her eyes and the memory of the fateful day slid into the dark corners of her mind. She snapped back to the present moment with her mom, dad, grandpa, Flynn, and Rena standing on the balcony as the waves crashed on the beach of Lake Michigan. She felt the warm sun on her cheek and the gentle breeze blowing through her hair. The car crash was in the past and she achieved her Olympic dreams. Cordelia looked at her Mom and Dad, and smiled.

"I have my family back," Cordelia broke the silence.

"Let's celebrate!" Albert smiled and rubbed his hands together.

38

The sun was sinking and the air was comfortably cool. By the time the guests arrived, Rena had her drum kit set up, and Flynn and Albert had decorated the indoor and outdoor spaces with balloons and streamers. Lit candles sat at the center of each table and flickered in the soft breeze.

A giant banner with "Congratulations to the Gold Medal Winners" written in big bold letters hung on the back wall of the banquet hall, and a giant cake sat on the long table below it. The colored frosting on the cake made Flynn's mouth water.

With everything set up, Flynn and Rena helped themselves to food and drinks from the buffet table. The circus performers were busy congratulating the guests of honor, filling the air with joyful conversation and laughter.

Out of the corner of his eye, Flynn noticed his parents arrive to the party. His dad carried a small cage with the white bunny scurrying around inside. Flynn jogged over to his dad and tapped him on the shoulder.

"You wanted me to bring this," Ray said with a puzzled look on his face.

"Yeah, yeah," Flynn said. He looked around to make sure Cordelia didn't see it. "It's a surprise present for Cordelia."

Ray handed the cage to Flynn.

Flynn grabbed the handle on top and said, "Follow me."

Flynn and his parents weaved through the tables. Cordelia

abruptly stopped talking to some guests when she saw the rabbit hopping around inside the cage. She ran over to Flynn.

"Is that Nixie?" Cordelia stammered. "How? Where did you find her?"

Flynn chuckled and asked, "Remember when I drew the poster for the circus?"

"Yeah," Cordelia said, raising her eyebrows.

"I used the photos from Albert's camper as a reference," Flynn said. "One of the pictures had you holding your bunny. The poster became real and I've been taking care of the rabbit ever since."

Cordelia opened the cage door and the rabbit jumped into her arms. She gave the fluffy bunny a gentle hug. A waiter stopped by with a half-eaten salad and placed the plate on the floor, smiling at Cordelia before he walked away. Cordelia smiled back and set the rabbit down. The bunny's whiskers twitched as it munched down on the carrots, celery, and lettuce.

"Thank you!" Cordelia said. "This was the second best present so far tonight."

"You're welcome," Flynn replied with a wide smile.

As Flynn and his parents walked away from Cordelia's table, Georgia leaned in close to Flynn's ear and said, "Cordelia and her family seem like nice people."

"They are, Mom," Flynn said.

Flynn and his parents joined Rena's family at their assigned table. While everyone ate, Flynn and Rena answered questions about Atlanta and what they'd seen at the Olympics.

Salvatore, who had changed into a nice suit, sat with Gala at one of the tables near the back of the room. His face glowed with pride. Holding Gala's hand, he leaned in and kissed her on the cheek.

Albert was busy talking to everyone, along with Cordelia and Marcel, who moved from table to table. They'd both dressed up for the occasion, and it seemed odd to see them without their circus outfits or Olympic uniforms. Both of them looked happy with the gold medals hanging around their necks.

Albert got everyone's attention by clanging a spoon against his glass. He stood and walked over to the front of the room near the sliding doors.

"If everyone is done eating, we'd like to move this party to the balcony for some music."

When people started to stand, Albert raised his hand.

"But before we go outside," Albert said. "Salvatore wanted to say a few words."

The guests whispered amongst themselves as Salvatore and Gala shuffled over to Albert and stood by his side. The room fell silent.

39

Salvatore raised his champagne glass and said, "I would like to make a toast to the winners, Cordelia and Marcel."

After a few moments of awkward silence, everyone raised their glasses and took a sip.

Salvatore fidgeted with his tie and cleared his throat. "I know I betrayed everyone's trust, but I hurt Cordelia the most." One by one, he looked at all of the circus performers. "I hope you'll give me the chance to make it up... To all of you."

Some of the circus performers nodded while others murmured amongst themselves. The tension eased a little in the room.

It took a lot of courage to get up in front everyone and apologize, Cordelia thought. She walked over to her dad and gave him a hug.

Cordelia turned around and announced to the guests, "Let's dance!"

Albert opened the slider door and waved everyone to move the celebration outside. The circus performers flowed out onto the balcony where all the musical instruments were set-up.

Rena had formed a band with some friends from college. On the weekends, they played together at friends' parties. Her band mates took their positions and started to play. One of her friends sang, another played the keyboard, and her other friend played the guitar.

Albert danced with Paula. Even Rena's parents danced to a song.

"You guys aren't dancing?" Flynn asked his parents.

"Not really my thing," Ray said.

"No, it's not," Georgia said with a wink.

Flynn stood and said, "Maybe you should play with the band instead."

"Play? With what?" Ray asked.

"I brought you a present." Flynn reached underneath table, brought out the violin case, and handed it to his dad.

Ray rubbed his forehead. "I don't know. I haven't played in so long and there are tons of people here."

"Oh come on," Flynn prodded. "I heard you practicing all the time when I was growing up."

Georgia nudged her husband.

"Okay," Ray muttered. "Maybe one or two songs."

~

Cordelia laughed as the band launched into a slow song. Marcel took her hand and led her to the dance floor, candlelight glinting off their medals as they moved.

The chatter fell silent and a hush passed through the crowd when Salvatore walked onto the dance floor and tapped Marcel's shoulder. Marcel straightened his posture as Salvatore spoke in his ear. Marcel nodded and went over to the balcony and leaned against the rail. Cordelia noticed how Marcel reacted with humbleness and kindness rather than anger.

Salvatore danced with Cordelia for the rest of the song, reminding her of how a normal dad would dance with his daughter.

There is nothing scary about my dad now, she thought.

"Cordelia," Salvatore said in solemn tone.

"Yes, Dad," Cordelia said.

Fighting back tears, he said, "I don't say this enough, but I'm proud of you."

Cordelia leaned back, hesitated for a moment, and then whispered, "Thanks, Dad."

She rested her head on his chest and when the song came to an end, she went to check on Marcel.

"Are you okay?" she asked, finding him leaning against the balcony railing.

"Yeah, I think so."

Cordelia noticed Marcel staring over at Salvatore.

"Are still angry with my dad?" she asked.

"A little," Marcel said. "But he's your dad and I want him to be in your life."

She hoped that things between Marcel and her father would heal over time.

"Thanks for understanding."

"You're welcome," Marcel said, mustering a smile.

"I have to talk to my grandpa for a minute, but after that, I'd like to continue our dance."

"I'd like that," Marcel beamed.

Cordelia patted his arm and then made her way over to where her grandpa was getting a glass of water from the refreshment table.

"Grandpa?"

"Yes, sweetie."

"Do you know what would make me happy?" Cordelia asked.

Albert glanced over at Marcel, Gala, and Salvatore. And then he gazed at all the smiling guests on the balcony.

"Did I miss something?" Albert asked.

"No, you didn't miss anything," She nudged him with her elbow. "But I think you should be up there with the band, too. It's time for you to play music again."

Albert looked down at the wood deck and his shoulders slumped. He mumbled something under his breath. The only word Cordelia heard was her grandmother's name, Elsa.

A purple glow reflected off Albert's clothing. Looking down at Albert's hand, Cordelia saw several small purple orbs floating around his wedding ring.

Cordelia grabbed Albert's arm, pointed, and asked, "Can you see it, too?"

He slowly nodded.

The orbs floated up to eye level and began to spin around

counter clockwise. Albert took a step back, pulling Cordelia with him. The orbs smashed together in a blind flash, dissolved into purple smoke, and hovered above the balcony. Slowly, the cloud formed into a person Cordelia hadn't seen in long time.

"Grandma Elsa," Cordelia whispered.

Elsa had long hair, piercing eyes, and a long flowing dress. Albert gasped, stepping forward to hug the ghost of his wife. His arms went right through her. She smiled sadly, reached out, and rested her hand on his shoulder. A tear streamed down her grandpa's cheek.

Elsa pointed to Cordelia's gold medal and said, "I knew you could do it. I'm so proud of you, Cordelia." Then she turned back to Albert. "Just for today, let go of your grief. Celebrate and play music again."

"I don't know." Albert whispered.

"I love hearing you play music," Elsa said. "Go on, I'm always listening, even when you can't see me."

Albert held his hands to his heart and nodded.

"I should go now," Elsa said. "It's your time. Enjoy the party, you both deserve it. And Albert..."

"Yes?"

"I love you," Elsa said.

"I love you, too," Albert said.

A second later, the purple smoke lost shape, drifted away with the wind, splashed into Lake Michigan, and blended with the blue waves.

"Wow," Cordelia whispered.

"Well then, it's time to show this band a thing or two," Albert said, running his fingers through his hair and straightening his suit.

He marched over to the edge of the stage and waited for the song to end.

Cordelia sought out Marcel. "Are you ready for a dance?"

"You bet." He took her hand and led her onto the dance floor.

Albert stepped onto the stage and spoke with Rena and the other band members. They each nodded in turn. A moment later, the keyboard player let Albert take her place. She grabbed a

Traveling Circus and the Skeleton Key

tambourine and everyone took their places.

His fingers slid across the keys and played a melody. He repeated a few chords, looked up, and raised his eyebrows. Rena nodded and started a beat that matched his tune. It took a minute, but the others all joined in.

The music started slow, but then progressed into an upbeat tempo. Soon, Cordelia was dancing and out of breath as the song finished.

"Want to sit down for a bit?" Marcel asked.

Cordelia nodded. They went to an empty table and sat, enjoying each other's company and watching Albert having a great time on stage.

After a few songs, Albert wiped his brow and held up his hands. "Okay, I need a break. I'll let the young people take over."

"I think we all could use a break. We'll be back in 15, folks," the lead singer announced over the microphone.

Rena and Flynn drifted over to the refreshment table. The other band members grabbed some soda and sat at a table together. The guests milled around on the balcony, talking and enjoying the view.

Albert went inside the banquet hall and came back out with the ammo box and beach towel under his arm. After speaking with Salvatore and Gala for a few minutes, they headed right for Cordelia and Marcel.

"What's your grandpa up to now?" Marcel asked.

"I don't know," Cordelia shrugged.

Carrying a beach towel, Albert and Cordelia's parents came to stand in front of them. Albert set the ammo box down on the table. A knot formed in Cordelia's stomach.

Salvatore opened the container, dropped the pocket watch inside, and slammed it shut, "I don't need this anymore."

"It's time we put the scroll, the pocket watch, and all that goes with it, back where it belongs, at the bottom of the lake, far away from our family," Albert said.

"I never want to see it again," Marcel grumbled.

"Me either," Cordelia said. "I'll put in back on the L.C. Woodruff."

Salvatore rested his hand her shoulder and said, "Good idea."

"I'll be back in a few," Cordelia said as she stood up from the table.

"I'll go with you," Marcel said. "We'll do this together, at least as far as the beach."

Taking her hand, Marcel escorted Cordelia down the balcony stairs and stepped onto the cool sand.

Albert called out from the balcony, "Good luck."

"Thanks," Cordelia said.

Marcel and Cordelia walked down the boardwalk toward Lake Michigan.

With the waves crashing on the beach, Cordelia handed her gold medal to Marcel and said, "Okay, turn around."

Marcel turned around and held up the large beach towel, giving her some privacy. She slipped out of her dress, waded into the water, and dove into the water with the ammo box.

"Be careful," he called after her.

"Thanks," she said.

Cordelia floated with the waves, closed her eyes, and imagined her legs turning into a tail. Her legs slowly fused together and scales protruded from her bare skin. She sank into the big lake and her gills opened underneath her jaw. Water entered her gills and oxygen pumped through her veins.

Opening her eyes, it took a few minutes to find her bearings as a mermaid again. Once she had her body under control, she swam in the direction of the shipwreck.

Can I find it again? she worried.

Her distress subsided when the purple orbs returned and guided her to the *L.C. Woodruff*. Approaching the ship, she saw it was buried on the edge of a sand bar. She swam inside the gaping hole in the main deck, weaved through the narrow halls, and dropped down to the bottom of the ship. With her bare hands, she dug a hole in the sandy floor and buried the ammo box. She stacked suitcases over the top.

Giving the ammo box a slow wave, she thought, *I hope I never see you again!*

She swam back to shore and raised her head above the water's surface. Her locket cover popped open and the purple orbs floated back inside.

Bright stars twinkled in the dark sky. Rena's drum beats echoed across the water. Marcel's dark shadow paced back and forth along the beach.

Cordelia imagined her tail turning back into legs as she swam into shallower water near Marcel. The green scales slid under her pink skin and her tail split into two legs and feet. When Marcel spotted her, he smiled, held up the towel, and averted his eyes.

"Thanks," she said, wading out of the lake.

She dried off, dressed, and draped the gold medal around her neck.

"You know," Cordelia drew out the words. "We don't have to go back to the party right away. Let's take a walk."

Marcel nodded, wrapped his arm around her shoulder, and gently squeezed. Surrounded by the music and the laughter of their friends, she closed her eyes, leaned in, and kissed him.

After a long embrace, Cordelia and Marcel walked along the shore of Lake Michigan. Holding her shoes in her hand, the wet sand squished between her toes and the pale moon smiled down on them.

She touched the shimmering gold medal with her fingertips and whispered, "I went for it. I fell a few times, but at least no one told me I couldn't do it."

The End
~

Book 1:
Traveling Circus
And the Secret Talent Scroll

The book follows the adventures of Cordelia as she discovers the mystery behind the Secret Talent Scroll.

Book 2:
Traveling Circus

The ringmaster, wielding a magic pocket watch that controls time, holds Flynn against his will. Flynn must find his inner courage to defeat the ringmaster and go home.

Book 3:
Traveling Circus
And the Skeleton Key

The conclusion to the Traveling Circus Series. Will Cordelia achieve her Olympic dream or remain forever stuck in a circus sideshow?

Made in the USA
Monee, IL
11 July 2023